Nesting Beasts

Naiche Lizzette Parker

Cover Design: Naiche Parker
Interior Design: Naiche Parker
ISBN: 978-0-578-70130-1

1. Poetry 2. Magical Realism 3. Anthology 4. Fiction
First Edition

for the girl I was

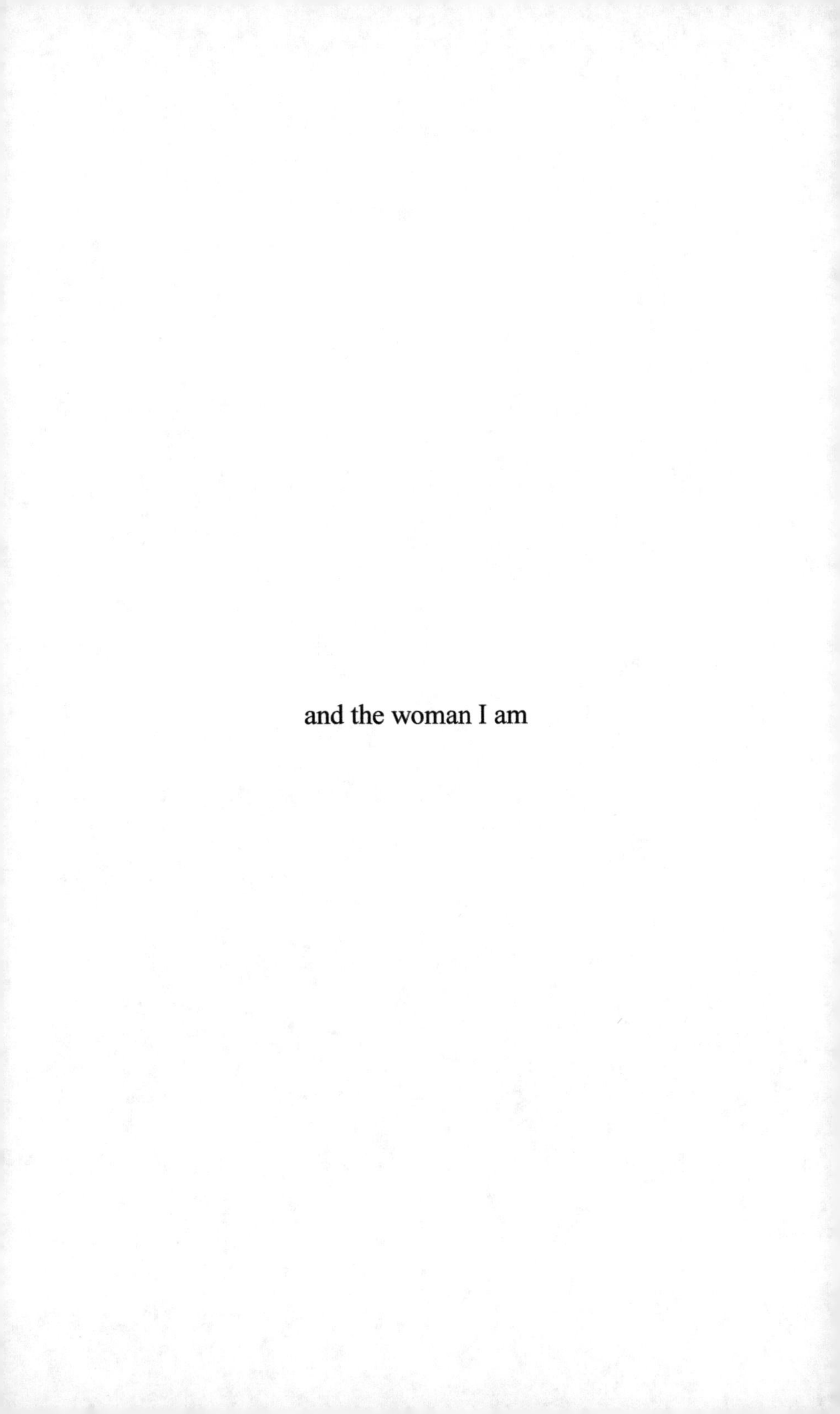

and the woman I am

TABLE OF CONTENTS

On Heartbreak

On Self

On Magic

INTRODUCTION

dolls, supermarket magazines,
weeds in the cracks of the concrete

Sometimes I think poetry is just a way to talk about
the same thing over and over again without tiring people.

how many motels, how many gas stations,
how many parking lots

A way to make begging beautiful.

apple orchards, astroturf,
the garden on the rooftop

All my life, everything was everything
except for what it actually was.

acorn fairies, boardwalks,
the bar and its liquor perfume

Poetry was about how much I could
lie while telling the truth.

how love is an audition, how love is a windowsill,
how love can never just be love

How I could hide while in plain sight.

———

    I've spent the first twenty-five years of my life chasing
after something that already lives inside of me. In my writing,
you'll often find the themes and symbols of reincarnation,

reflections, matryoshka dolls, and past and future selves waltzing across the ballroom of what time does to us. Everything is a compass pointing back to oneself.

This life so far has been a slow but gorgeous realization that we are the containers of our own fates, and that in our bodies live communities of selves that must be protected in order to tell the magnificent stories of who we were, who we are, and who we will be.

I didn't always think this way. I traveled scarily far out of myself before I thought to look within. I dreamt of becoming some other girl, cooler or more beautiful than who I was. I lusted over something that I believed was beyond myself and searched for it in costumes, countries, and other people. In my first three poetry books, I see a girl yearning— for magic, strength, and love.

I am here now to show her that she had those things all along.

You'll find many of my favorite works from *Paper and Bones*, *Rabbit Holes*, and *More Than Anything* inside of *Nesting Beasts*. I liked the idea of those three girls and the woman I am now living in one place. This book is my matryoshka doll; the deeper you fall into these poems and stories, the more you'll understand that growth is a long and complicated tale. You see her on a shelf, and she's lovely, but the entire story lives inside of her. When you think you have her figured out, there is yet another, smaller doll to unearth, hidden but still there. The things we once did and people we used to be nest inside of us forever and play an integral role in keeping us whole.

I can't tell you how many times I read back my own writing and am exhausted with myself. Being a poet isn't always romantic. *"Gods and monsters, pain and heartbreak,*

*stars and California roads, daddy issues and boys who are
walking cigarettes, blah, blah, blah."* I watch my history
unfold through my own work and wish that I would get a grip
and maybe take up embroidering or a sport instead. I am not
always emotional and serious and bleeding out. I like to laugh
and curse and be brash, sometimes annoying. I enjoy the
lightness as much as I do the heaviness of everything. I think
shallow water has a bad reputation. I like to sing at the top of
my lungs as much as I like whispering into the night because
I detest the thought of being just one kind of person.

(Yes, to answer your question, I am a Gemini.)

But I am not me without all of this. Every poem has
been an excavation, an expedition further within me. Even the
fictional short stories you'll read in this book will speak my
most vivid truths between the lines. My words have helped me
understand the past as I lived it and invent my future as I see
it, simultaneously making it easier to exist in the present.

It was never about what I didn't have but what I didn't
see in myself. I no longer say that I want to be kinder. I want
all of my kindness to be known. I no longer claim that I am
looking for my great love. It lives in me, and I decide who I
want to experience it with. I no longer want to be someone
else. I am longing to get to know myself.

I hope this book will inspire you to know yourself.

I hope that you go forth unafraid to open up and
embrace what lives inside.

I hope that you become a home for all of your nesting
beasts.

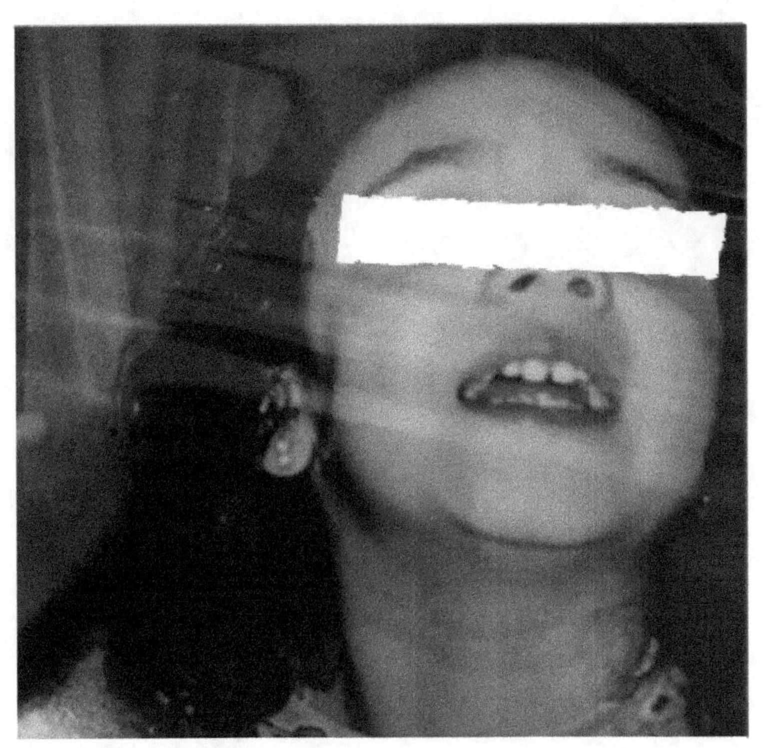

on childhood

SNOW GLOBES

inside of this one,
my father is still Poseidon,
and I am running towards him
in the ocean and who he is
hasn't put its hands
on what I think of him.

inside of this one,
the house is warm
and has all its eyes
and all its mouths open,
and I hang over its windowsill lashes
and paint on the walls
because we'll live here forever,
where else?

inside of this one,
I am young
and still believe in impossible things
like a face in the moon
like love without caveats
like myself
and like you.

inside of this one,
we have just met and the bar is warm
and your hands are new
and it's the last kiss
before I know it is the last
and who I am is still a stranger
to what you think of me.

inside of this snow globe,
I am just kneeling

in front of another one,
some glass altar,
some idol of fantasy,
watching icy flakes fall
but outside it is July
and everything is burning.

a nutcracker slides a lever
to open his own mouth,
to tell me
that memory is a prison,
that the stars as we once saw them
and as we now see them
can look the same
but tell a different story.

that even if I could
learn to trap time,
I still couldn't turn it
into the truth.

AT CONFESSION, THEN TEN HAIL MARYS

i. bless me father, for I have sinned.

ii. bless me father, for I have longings immortal as
Cleopatra's. I think I am obsessed with strangeness.

iii. bless me father, for when I was younger, I had a
recurring dream of my parents and I driving along a cliffside,
then being devoured by wolves. there were four of them
and three of us. I pretend not to know what this means.

iv. bless me father, for I have been thinking about
corn husk dolls. an army of them, faceless and somehow
smiling, draped and dangling in the sun.

v. bless me father, for I am addicted to sudden downpours.
of rain and in my life. drowning without the urgency of
drowning.

vi. bless me father, for I have faced no horror like the one
fashioned by my own mind.

vii. bless me father, for in another dream,
only I was devoured.
only I was the wolf.

viii. bless me father. bless me father. bless me father.
I keep inventing pain so that I can feel at home.
I keep unravelling my repentance like shoelaces,
stumbling over my growth. I keep—

ix. bless me father, for I will sin again.

SAYING HELLO TO GOD

Mass starts,
and I show up ten years late
with a red dress on and a few scars.

there's a homeless man sleeping on the back pew,
and Jesus cries some mosaics for him;

I don't know where to begin, so I just say,
"sorry God, for not calling
or being kinder
and praying without the Our Father."

my parents never baptized me,
I guess I was born with a pair of eyes
that asked too many questions;
wanted to see the map and not just the directions.

I say,
"the years have been long,
but I'm no stranger to penance
do you have time for a quick confession?"

I was a matchstick girl,
and the bible told me not to burn bridges;
no Hail Mary could prepare me
for the cruelty of adolescence—
no Act of Contrition.

I can still recite the eight Beatitudes in my sleep,
but all I know about myself is that
you made me in your image.
thank Jesus for wearing thorns
but not my reflection.

all they taught me was to worship,
and I did—
nicotine, caffeine, boys with smiles like both.
(I was looking for the messiah)
you said do unto others as you would to yourself;
so, I tore apart.

this girl cut her fingers on the stars for me once,
this boy cut me with them,
but only one of them is called sinning.
ten years, the good book—
I guess I'm still just confused.

God, I never asked to be a martyr
or to feel guilt in my freedom
maybe all that bad is just bad,
maybe I can decide on what's good.

don't get me wrong,
I still think of you even when I don't visit,
I still feel heaven in my bones.
on the cusp of my death, it's like an itch,
I still fold my hands to pray.

I guess you lost me so that I could find myself,
and I'll be damned if that isn't called love—
even if this house makes it impossible
for us to be together.

sorry God,
for always running.
but the service is starting,
the homeless man is leaving
to make space for the true believers.

I guess I have too many questions.

ROSALINE

you do not realize that
you aren't Juliet
until Juliet enters Act One.

at the climax of your story,
you are just his prologue,
preamble,
preparing the clay for another's hands.

when you were eight years old,
he used to break your dolls in half.
(things were uncomplicated then;
you weren't allowed to play with swords)

he said,
"have it your way, Rosaline.
see? like this.
someday girls will be dying
to be with me."

you never loved him,
you claim.
you are just tired
of being a backstory.
we are all just tired
of being backstories.

during the processions,
you sat by the window and watched.
once they were in the ground,
it rained,
the blood was washed away,
and you could not see where one house ended

and the other began.

your mother was a cold woman.
her hand on your shoulder was gone
before it got there.

"that could have been you," she said.

you still don't know if this makes you lucky
or not.

IN FORMER LIVES

in former lives,
my mother is the willow tree
that droops in the backyard to keep me alive.
all bruised fruit spilling what juice it can,
my shelter, my Demeter,
the dormant volcano somehow meant to burn
and be a place to rest.

my brother is the first living, breathing rabbit
I see outside of a picture book.
the dandelion clinging onto the thorns
of the rose I am born as
in a wild garden.
the old man whispering soft stories
upon the roof of my tenement in a time of blood and war.

my father is everything that ever kills me.
a ravenous storm, a poison berry, a vulture—
and mine, the first fresh face in the desert.
other natural disasters that can't help what they are.

my best friend is a strawberry still demanding to ripen
after everything that happened in Eden.
my twin tree in a forest of fairytales,
ashes to ashes, branches to branches,
holding hands as roots when the men came to bare us.

my lover is the elixir and the downfall.
the bolt of lightning in 1909 that should have killed me
but brought me back to life.
the bleeding war mate, the windowsill sparrow,
the faithful knight, the gas station glance
I have never seen before
and recognize every time.

others are stray stars that appear above the highway
when I've needed to feel close to the impossible.
one Brutus, one Judas,
in whichever chapters were titled betrayal.
armies that stood behind me with
swords or sticks or words for weapons,
erupting sunsets that then had names and faces
the next go-around,
one cast and centuries of costumes.

each time I am born the same:
small and screaming for the loss of them.
each time I am born the same:
in search again.

HOMECOMING

revisiting my childhood home is a clenched fist.

in the hands of its second family,
all the flowers we planted that summer have died.

when their walls howl,
when their floors creak,
I wonder if my parents' screams are still echoing.
I wonder if there is a universe where
we are still sitting down to dinner.

when they think they are being haunted by ghosts,
I wonder if they are right.

I pay my respects to
this cemetery of all the mothers fathers children
we tried to be,
of all the selves we wore
that never fit.

the shutters look like the eyes
on a face
I've forgotten the name of.

we drive away from the doorframe
on which I once carved
"forever."

NEVER

i.
here is a secret:
stories don't change;
we just begin to tell them differently.

ii.
Dorothy is wearing black gingham
and stomps a cigarette out on a yellow line
fading along the pavement
when the traffic sign summons her, emerald green.
around her is a landscape of places
that shrink when you hit twenty-one
and get the fuck out of town
and change the subject on the phone
when your aunt asks if you're still having those dreams.

iii.
there were seven of them once,
so naturally there are six seats open
if you don't count the casket.

iv.
Peter and Wendy are arguing by a gravestone,
and Dorothy can't hear it,
but just by the look in the girl's eyes,
she can tell it's one they've had a million times—
like if you know a lost boy too long, he becomes a lost man
and all that charming becomes cheating,
and life on the windowsill isn't as endearing,
and there she is realizing the mistake
of making a home out of an escape.

v.
it's a quiet procession.

Dorothy sits beside Crow,
still dressed like a lumberjack and tripping over his own feet.
her first real friend,
maybe her only real friend,
and the boy she would have married if either of them
had been brave enough to call it that.
but neither of them had ever asked to be brave.

vi.
Dorothy never had a stable home,
and Crow's father would call him stupid
but say it with his fist,
so they would run away together to find what they were
missing in those neon signs off the highway
or each other.
when they turned sixteen, they would get high
and he would feel brilliant and she would finally belong
if only until dawn, and she will remember this tonight,
after the funeral, when he's got his tongue in her mouth
behind the Oz Diner,
and Crow will say, "I hate you
for leaving me in this fucking town,"
and Dorothy will joke, "there's no place like home."

vii.
she'll remember:
habits thrive on their own absence.

viii.
Alice is the most fucked up out of all of them
but won't admit it.
Dorothy's heard rumors about those red-rimmed eyes,
that too long spent down a rabbit hole
and you'll forget which way is up,
and even your rock-bottom will have a rock-bottom.
she's dressed like a child frozen in time

and leaves a rose for the dearly departed,
cries beside her roommate Hatter,
who bartends every night at The White Rabbit
and sells drugs on the side.

ix.
no one shows up except for the old gang.
they bring the sweet irrelevant nothings
that only childhood friends can offer
to a body older than the life they knew—
how she'd bake them all cookies,
and those made great fucking edibles (*sorry pastor*),
how she took care of her grandmother
even when things got scary,
even when what comes with old age
began to lurk behind her eyes and teeth,
how she wanted what they all wanted:
a ticket out of town or inside a dream,
the stories they'd tell themselves,
how leaving is just another way of hiding.

x.
the priest clears his throat.
"we gather here to remember
our beloved
Red Riding."

DIVORCE

dear Mom and Dad,
both of you have asked me
about time travel, fleeting conversations
in the car about
which moment in history I'd go back to,
which disaster I'd stop,
which lips I wouldn't kiss,
which war I would end.

I always laugh and turn to the window,
whisper,
I wouldn't change a thing.

my personal philosophy is that everything
happens for a reason, that every bone broken
is already one on the mend,
that the world is always exactly where it needs to be,
spinning whichever way it needs to spin.

I'm sorry for lying.
at age sixteen, I promised I wouldn't ever again,
but while you change the song on the radio
and take the next left,
I am already fifteen years behind you.

the food is ready, and my school uniform
is drying, the air smells like mowed grass,
detergent, and both of you.
my brother hasn't been born yet,
he's just some north star in the distance,
promising everything and nothing at all.

today is a good day.
the sun is just setting,

Mom puts down her sword,
and Dad takes off his armor.
we fold our hands together and unbreak our hearts.

we dine in half-silence, half-memory,
and I collect bits and pieces of what you both are
to eat for dessert.

after,
Elvis takes pity and sings to your terrible dancing,
I laugh and my heart swells as I watch you,
already forgetting what I never thought
would be so hard to remember.

the future is just folklore,
we are here and now,
a triad of thieves and lovers and fools,
I fall in love with you two first,
the rest of the world later,
the beginning and end of my being.

you kiss me on the forehead
and clear off my plate.
one day,
we will break more than just bread.

dear Mom and Dad,
here's your answer:
I would just sit down to dinner.
because you don't know what you're feeling
until you never feel that way again.

FOR THE PERSON MY BROTHER WILL MARRY

he is so good.

I do not say this because he is my blood and bone
or because he was the only plant that ever
grew in my hands.

he is just good.

the sort of good that doesn't have an addendum
the sort of good that makes watching the news easier.
the sort of good that carries others.

with him and for him,
I have survived the bombs.
with him and for him,
I have woken up for another fight.

I do not just give you my brother.
I give you my reason.

I have watched him grow from smile to soul to boy to man,
but in my heart,
we are still children making tents out of shadows,
we are still the casualties of being,
we are still strung together like tin cans.
we are still the sounds that drowned out the screaming.

and still, he is good.

PERSPECTIVE

when I was younger,
there was a creature that lived
underneath my bed,
scratched at the hardwood,
growled in its slumber,
eyes yellow and
fur creeping
while I was sleeping.
sometimes,
I was afraid.
other times,
it would sing me songs
in a language I didn't know,
speak of a world floors deep
where the darkness kept its vacation home.
we became friends,
the bond of solitude,
the company of alone.
I only saw its face once when
I was twenty-five
and visiting my childhood home.
I called after it,
"monster under my bed!"
this would be the first and only time,
a flash of fur that went to hide.
it blinked at me and said,
"you have always been
the monster under mine."

THE IMPOSSIBLE SCALE

I try never to belittle anyone's pain. Think of the impossible scale to measure all things. If life has ever made sense to you, you're either God or a liar.

September 11th arrives, and I feel the saddest I have on this day since 2001. Dread fills me. When people ask the obligatory question, where I was when it happened (*here, home, New York City, just six, the classroom, smoke on the television screen, call my mother, she works right around there, she had taken the day off, call my grandmother, where is my father, let's sit on the floor, let's wait, let's—*), one of those impossible scales to measure all things, I don't feel like answering.

A month later, I visit a statue called Double Check Businessman that's right by Zuccotti Park. He used to live in the World Trade Center and somehow survived the attack with barely a scratch. When I was a little girl, I would call him my husband. I played with him almost every weekend because my grandmother would take me to the Twin Towers almost every weekend.

He is just as I remembered, and I don't know if that makes me feel better or worse.

I suppose I expected him to seem smaller after all these years.

But it's me who feels two feet tall.

on home

FLIGHTY

sometimes
I don't want to live here anymore.
the girls I used to be are
everywhere in this city,
taunting me,
reminding me of how much
and how little I have changed,
begging me to slip back into their skin.

PLAYING CARDS

Did you know that there are enough lost playing cards on the sidewalks and streets, sewers and crevices of New York City that if you looked hard enough over an entire lifetime, you are likely to find an entire deck? I didn't know what to do with this information when an ex-boyfriend told me years ago, so inconsequential but suddenly meaning so much to me. I see them all the time now—the Ace of Spades mingling with wrappers and cigarette butts, the Two of Clubs crossing the street with the wind—like receipts of trickery.

You don't notice at all and then it's all you can—like the influx of couples that seem to be doing flash mobs at every grocery store, train station, movie theater now that you're single. Like the passing of time and how many fancy coffee shops are suddenly everywhere.

Lately, I've been waking up in the middle of the night, anxious about where the years went. The decade is almost over. I count cloudy memories like sheep, but I still can't rest.

Morning runs and lungs on fire, the echoes of Bachata music and thick taste of corn meal, graveyards and iced coffee, euphoria, trash television and old television, the best kinds of dates with the worst kinds of people, bad hair days, good hair days, a first kiss asking to be my last, a room transforming into a million fantasy lands made of light, one fake red wedding dress and the howling full moon, my name as a spell, Mood Ring and making out with a marble bust.

Just more lost playing cards, I guess.

Somewhere among them, an entire deck.

SUMMER IN NEW YORK

this summer I want the lower east wildebeests
and their platinum horns
to start a rumpus within me.

I will stand beneath an August downpour
until my clothes melt and my skin melts
and my bones become concrete,
which you know here is charming,
which you know here is a living, breathing thing—
hot and pulsing and vibrating
and holding all the blood and fights
and first kisses and debris,
absorbing all that we shed,
more earth to us than grass.

this summer I want to bc kissed
in every neighborhood I've been hurt.

I want to scream and laugh and cry in every car
of the train my ex-boyfriend takes,
hoping then he will finally hear me,
hoping then for a way to say goodbye.

I want to fall back in love
with this city that refuses to be loved
or must be loved and knows it.

I want to soak in
everything that once tried to drown me.

I want this kingdom of grit to crown me —
bodega princess
East River angel
patron saint of city girls.

THE JUNGLE BOOK

it's dangerous to raise your kids in the city.
we become concrete, callous things.
howling at the fluorescence because
it's the closest thing we'll get to starlight.

so starved for daylight that we'll
call anything pure.

we scream at the skyline
like iron beasts,
climb up lamppost moons.

born from leather, skin like stone,
we are always just waking up,
always waiting for the train,
always wiping away that Big Apple blood.

finding bruises
from nights that we can't remember.
here, summer still looks like December.

ahead of time
and losing our minds,

there is a restlessness that we were born with:
never lose,
never sleep,
never die.

it is a terrifying thing,
to live where everyone else wants to be,
at the end of the world,
nowhere left to run,
nothing more to see.

ARTIFICES

The Princesse de Broglie has a secret.

She admits so to A Girl Asleep because, of course, she is asleep, and that is the best kind of person to tell a secret.

It is Thursday at dusk, and the Metropolitan Museum of Art is shutting its doors and stretching its arms, preparing for evening. The janitor spews his final whistle, and then the paint begins to peel. Not from the walls, but from the paintings.

The stallions at The Horse Fair gallop from oil paint to stale air, buck at each other in competition for the grains shaking off of the Wheat Fields of Cypress.

Madame X is portrait then woman, red-blooded and yearning, heels clicking across the galleries to collect her posse—Elizabeth Farren who knows everything so shouldn't be trusted but *should* be friended, Fragonard's Love Letter who she calls Frag, mostly because the name is ugly and the subject is prettier than her, and Celia, who's a bit modern for her taste. Monsieur Aublet stretches his arms out of his portrait to offer them Cassatt's lilacs, and Madame X sneers.

The statues soften, too. Harlequina and Little Dancer of Fourteen Years twirl through the growing crowd of breathing artworks. Saint John the Baptist goes pliant and preaches to some ceramics who won't listen.

Already, The Princesse is exhausted. It used to be that only some of the paintings knew their potential. A handful of them would slip from their acrylic prisons and pour over the most delicious-looking still-lives like menu pictures, feast upon Peale's cake and Ream's fruit whilst lying about the museum's furniture exhibits, kiss in the alcoves tucked by the staircases, and swim in The Temple of Dendur.

They aren't the people in their paintings, she knows that much. They aren't possessed by desperate ghosts. They are their own. Their spirits are new, swallowing up the words whispered at them by art critics, students, couples, and curious kids throughout the day—

—gorgeous technique on this one—

—maybe I should choose something more modern for the project; if I get another C I'm totally screwed—

—should we walk through the park after this—

—so yeah, I told him I wouldn't fuck him until he took that goddamn Star Wars poster off...oh, sorry...Jesus, I thought we were at the fucking Met, not the Vatican—

—I. Want. Lollipop. Now. I. Want—

—then regurgitating them as their own thoughts come evening. They were once a small family, a society, a secret club. She and the Madame had been friends, even. She'd regularly babysat for Roulin. The Handsome One had kissed her in The Great Hall. Her first kiss.

And then, the masses. The Princesse doesn't know why or how it happened. All of a sudden, the halls were filled and hot and chaotic with works of art demanding being. Perhaps the life of them had roused it in others.

"Do I bow for The Princesse so that she can get out of my way?" Madame X snarls now.

The Princesse purses her lips. Madame X stands a foot taller than her. Her hair is gorgeously arranged. One strap of her dress slips from her shoulder.

"To what do I owe this pleasure?" The Princesse shifts aside and Madame passes her, Elizabeth, Frag, and Celia tailing her in formation.

"Your misfortune," Madame yawns. "Now if you'll excuse me—"

The Princesse hesitates only a second before reaching for Madame's hand. "Why don't we go for one last swim at Dendur? For old time's sake."

Madame snatches her hand away, gives The Princesse a cutting glare and rolls her shoulders back as the trio of ladies behind her snicker.

"LAST swim, de Broglie?" she scoffs. "Before what? Are you going on vacation?"

The Princesse laughs. Around them, fruits and broken table legs stumble from their frames. Cherub angels steal the hats from soldiers and dangle them out of reach, hiccupping with laughter near the ceiling.

"Not quite, but perhaps we can," The Princesse muses. "Let's get away from this mess like we used to. Collect the coins at the bottom of the pool, stare up at the real night sky. You and I, just like before."

Madame's shoulder falls, her other strap with it. Her resolve, with it.

"I could entertain a dip," she murmurs.

"Hm," Frag chirps beside her, "so could I."

"Not YOU," Madame hisses, waving the woman away, taking The Princesse by the elbow, and dragging her through the crowd.

The Princesse laughs as Madame whisks her through the quiet halls of Egypt. They pause at the cusp of Dendur and smile at each other a moment before jumping straight into the icy pool. The women splash at one another, Madame's slinky dress clinging to her like an oil spill, The Princesse's elaborate dress puffing out and forcing her afloat.

"Perhaps I *did* miss this," Madame admits when they're quiet and drying and staring through the glass at Central Park in its slumber, the stars blazing through the pockets of night above it. "The quiet."

The Princesse smiles.

"Close your eyes," she whispers to her old friend, shifting until their heads are just barely touching and the strands of their hair are almost entangled. "Let's enjoy this."

Some hours later, Madame wakes.

The Princesse is gone, the sun is rising, and she must get back to her canvas. Madame races through the halls of the museum so quickly that she doesn't realize she isn't wearing her own signature black dress, the one that so many patrons lean too closely to get a real look at it.

The one that sets off alarms.

She's wearing a blue gown. That of royalty.

In the American wing, a number of people are slipping back into their paintings and the worlds within them. The Wagon jumps from the floor and loses dimension, frozen still within its sketchy Alleyway. The pointing Trapper directs Annie C. Hyde back to her black and white portal.

But one frame is missing.

"Where the FUCK is my canvas?" Madame screeches, chest pounding at the sight of the blank spot on the wall where her home should be. Sun pours into the Met now. She doesn't have much time. "And where the hell is that BITCH, de Broglie?"

Abandoned, she races through the galleries and other wings, nearly knocking over a few Roman statues in pursuit of sanctuary. She begs a few murals to help her in but, of course, they don't respond.

When she finally stumbles into the Robert Lehman collection, Madame is sobbing.

One painting is missing its subject.

Madame X stares down at the blue dress hanging from her own curves, up at the waiting gilded frame in realization.

She clenches her fists.

———

A few weeks later, a content woman wearing a blue coat over a slinky black dress sips her coffee on the steps of the Met, awaits its opening hour. She gulps it down and hands the empty cup to a security guard who tosses it away before letting her through.

"Are you a resident?" the ticket woman asks.

"You could say so." The woman in the blue coat smiles and hands her a twenty-dollar bill.

She makes her way forward, that familiar maze of halls at the museum's core, knowing that somewhere behind the walls, in its archives, its veins, there is now a stolen painting tucked away in the trench coat of de Monvel's The

31

Handsome One where there wasn't one before, its subject caught in a permanent wink. The woman blows a kiss for him.

Within Robert Lehman, her eyes fall to a familiar gold frame. The yellow chair. The gorgeous dress.

"I swear, Amy, this has been my favorite painting since college," she overhears a woman remark, "there's something up about the face. I can't put my finger on it. She looks different. Angrier."

The Princesse, just a woman now, like all women with secrets, hides her smile with her palm.

A Girl smiles in her Sleep.

LAST SUMMER ON THE ROOFTOP

last summer on the rooftop, Father Time put his fingers in my mouth, reached into my throat and into my chest, and yanked out my fear.

last summer on the rooftop, we got drunk and the sky fell. we all thought we were fist-fighting with the stars.

last summer on the rooftop—the strange boys across the hall, the thick nights, the vibrance, the laze, the freedom, the New York of it all.

last summer on the rooftop, making bright and burning spectacles of ourselves, shouting and stretching out beyond our bodies. for just a moment, we were the constellations, and the galaxies were our onlookers, learning the stories of what we did in desperation, in solitude, in love with a city and begging it not to forget us.

ODE TO THE NEW YORK CITY BAR

you lawful, godless country,
you mecca for missing things,
you orphanage for abandoned hearts,
where the skin is electric,
where everything begins and nothing starts.

the iMessage bacchanal,
get here, get young.
learn the language of apathy
or to speak in tongues.

I could wear you as a perfume—
I could bottle you up.
linoleum and bleach,
cigarette smoke and leather,
Chanel no. 5, some growing addiction,
and maker's mark.

I want your tired, your poor,
your thirsty masses.
an aphrodisiac for night-crawlers,
a siren's song summoning
all your life's regrets.

as in emptiness that becomes of getting too full,
maybe I saw too much of myself in you,
a child dressing her dolls up for the dark toy bin,
screaming just to be heard saying
that you hadn't said anything.

PUNCHLINE

love is like
the MTA

we are always
being held
momentarily

THERE'S NO PLACE LIKE HOME

We go out at night, and time doesn't exist. We look like glitter, innocent enough but sticking everywhere, then fleeing for the next best thing.

Every bar in New York City isn't as cool as it thinks it is, but that's the best part of it.

I eat pizza on the sidewalk and announce to one black cat and a food delivery guy that "this is my tradition!"

My lipstick has retired for the night and remnants of it make it seem like I've just been kissed.

Which is true, I've just been kissed.

No part of any of this belongs to tomorrow.

(Does this make sense?) I've always wanted to be this young.

SEASON'S GREETINGS

for those who saw broken lights
at the end of October
and thought of the holiday season.

store windows,
cranberry sauce,
kitchen knives.

for those who cannot stomach the holly:
all that green and red, moss and blood.

for those who thrive on the lights,
swallow them whole
to find warmth in themselves.

for those who need December.
for those who pretend there are eleven months.

for those who celebrate all
or one
or none.

for those waiting on the corner of heartbreak,
present still wrapped.

for those who seek the pine
only because
it's how they remember the mountains.

whether it was as simple as
a snowfall
or as difficult as a blizzard:
thank you for surviving.
and to all a good night.

on pain

A SECRET

you are afraid that something bad will happen,
but each night, the future steps into your dreams
with her shoulders bare and hands ready
to distort your worry, whispering
that you cannot stop something bad from happening
by thinking about it all the time—
that it will have to happen someday,
like death and rot and sleep,
and that when it happens,
it will not matter if you knew it would,
just that it happened after all.

SELF

it's not the pain
it's the pleasure
of healing over what used to hurt
somehow recovery is an addiction too

I once
kept myself awake for thirty-six hours
bleary-eyed aching and delusional
for the rest that came after
I swear
I have never fallen asleep the way
I did that night
my sheets were all ocean pulling me under
my body was heavy
I was anchored to the earth
it was euphoric

as a child
I would never use a public restroom
I would tornado my room in fits of rage
then go placid picking it up
those who have only known chaos
cannot comprehend doing things the easy way
enjoying things for how simple they can be
I am all rock-bottom
being rewarded with the come-up
like my mother and her mother and her mother
I only know how to make things better
and measure on the scale of what could be worse

here I am,
experiment 636
a rat
that has already learned the difficult route

to the cheese and won't budge
I am not insulting myself
we just have nothing nice to say to the
garbage collector who collects their own garbage
the
firefighter who lit the match
the
doctor stitching their own wound
is a hero not a hero when they
played a role in their tragedy?

I am Munchausen
I am mother
I am child

perhaps one day
I will not have to die
to feel alive

UNTITLED IS THE TITLE

I think that when you're drifting,
you feel that any anchor might save you.

and it does.

but after a while,
it just becomes another thing
keeping you from moving forward.

another thing
keeping you from the shore.

> sometimes I wonder how much things
> actually hurt me,
> and how much I had to convince myself
> that they did in order to walk away.

> pain can be a trap,
> but enough pain
> can become freedom.

FROM THE TREE

which are worse?
the days that I worry I'll end up like you
or the ones I worry I won't?

when I was a little girl, I dressed up as the white rabbit,
tried to trick you into falling down a different hole.

Alice, your wonderland
is not mine.

I know,
this monster isn't you either,
but she has your eyes.
she wears your clothes;
the estranged sister who has come
to borrow your car and crash it,
to borrow your life and crash it.

I know,
you aren't what you drink either,
but sometimes I feel like I've found a home
at the bottom of your glass,
convinced that if Orpheus could do it,
I can find you, too.

this love affair we have with red wine
and prosecco is a nightmare.
and a taboo, perhaps,
because it's screwing us both.

I see you through a wine bottle mosaic,
hear you through the language of apologies,
the things you're sorry you said last night.

at parties,
they used to look at us,
chaos and its reflection
caught through smashed glass.
we'd finish each other's sentences,
and they'd say that the apple doesn't fall far from the tree.

it doesn't.

it falls into a glass of its own.

TOXIC

we never pretended that
Bonnie and Clyde were a love story,
or wore our gore and called ourselves romantics,
just like you can't rip out my heart
and call it a valentine.

we weren't young gods,
just monsters at the dawn of our own destructions,
howling at each other with anything but our voices,
shooting one another with everything but guns.

the liquor store at midnight
loved us better than daylight;
back against the pillars in the parking lot,
sometimes wondering if you wanted to know my blood
better than you knew me.

you're smoking two cigarettes at once,
and I'm pumping gas in broken heels;
there's this song playing about the things we do for love,
and you smile.

flashback to the fourth grade, and I'm asking
my teacher how Eve must've felt,
that so much of her was just Adam,
as if this isn't the end of my beginning.
as if I haven't become the girl
whose backbone is a boy.

sticky sheets and something too ugly
to dream up as a child.
the sun says hello, but I'm feeling hungover.
last night, our fight,
I drank too much of you.

we don't pretend that we are a love story,
or wear all these scars like we earned them.
the night just creeps in and sets fire to
all our sins before the low whisper of,
"if I die here tonight,
please don't tell my mother about
the way I loved you."

PATRON SAINT OF DISAPPOINTMENT

I am not the saint,
I am the prayer.

so do not mistake my light
for divinity.

I am some neon sign
imitating the moon across the highway.

I beg that you do not
turn me into a god.

I bleed often and by my own hand.
I squint under the sun.
I will disappoint you.

you will learn to love me for rattling the stars,
then to hate me for forgetting their order.

MASOCHIST

I only know a love that hurts.

I have my hand on the stove,
my head in the lion's mouth,
your blade in my stomach,
whispering,
"thank you.
I was hungry."

I am the sword swallower's daughter;
taking your sharpness
and making a living,
mistaking all of this
for a gift

when you meant
for it to kill me.

WHEN THEY ASK ME ABOUT YOU

every person has a Doctor Frankenstein.
I came to you on ice,
clean for molding.
I came to you for the ripening.
I came to you for the programming.

you cut me open and
switched around my brain and heart.
there was blood.

(I was your peach)
there was bruising.

Mary Shelley told it best:
to me, you were god.
to you, I was body parts.

to this day, I am still writing you out of my code.
your voice still lives in the back of my throat.

VIOLENT DELIGHTS

right before the kill,
you kiss me.
warning: this is ugly.

once, you called me a butterfly.
oh. I get it, I get it,
in some places they eat insects.

warning: this is gory.
this is a very scary story.

you've unpeeled me,
but you're still not happy.

I am paper,
begging you to cut your fingers on what I am.

we are someone else's blood,
we are gum under the desks,
hot rain, a mess.

you say you want to drown in me
or drown me—
I didn't quite hear you.

when did you forget I was human?
when did you become my Manson?
when did we start calling crazy for each other
a compliment?

right before the kill you tell me,
story has it people fall in love with their deaths.

baby, your pretty face
looks just like the end.

HOW TO LOSE HER

let her pour her heart out
without raising your glass,

remind her with every missed call
that girls in love finish last.

tell her who you are,
then shed your snakeskin come fall.

promise her everything,
then break the pinky off.

lure her in with love,
then leave her on the hook.

say how she shines hurts your eyes,
so you don't bother to look.

turn the purity of her love
into a dirty game you like to play.

win her over as one man,
and then, like a magician!
suddenly change.

see her learn herself
through all she bore
and what remains.

congratulations,
she knows her worth.
now watch her walk away.

TO MY FATHER'S NEW DAUGHTER

forgive me, I cannot love you.
not just yet, maybe not ever.

we are two different legends with the same origin myth,
we fear the same god, but your bible is not mine.
the binomial experiment—no mercy on the first try.

we share the only part of myself that I hate,
the blood that I hope is leaking out of me
with every paper cut.

forgive me, I cannot hate you.
not now and maybe not ever.

this first draft has finished herself, survived him as he was
so you could be loved by somebody else.

and in learning to lose me,
perhaps he will hold onto you tighter
or breed another fighter.

perhaps you will know me through the breadcrumbs
I left as a trail out of these woods.
perhaps when they tell you that you have our father's eyes
it will mean something good.

perhaps I can love you
through what dents I ever made in his armor.
perhaps this is not a matter of sequels,
what shines, what's new,
and although we cannot walk together,
I can hand over my girlhood like a baton.

perhaps I raised him
to raise you.

A GAME OF CLUE

in our family home,
with your suitcase packed.

at the bottom of the wine glass,
with my childhood on the line.

under the desk,
with my leg shaking beneath your hand.

in the back stairwell,
with my heart between my legs.

at prom,
with a drink.

after I wrote my first book,
with my words lost on you.

right here, right now,
with my life in your hands.

and you?
playing catch.

on love

CONFESSIONAL

I've always promised to be honest: I am thirsting for love.

So I part my lips for my own fingertips. I wear red. I summon every god of affection from every religion, even inventing a few of my own. I kneel at an altar to my own heart. I slow dance with old memories and paint masks to give them new faces.

They are not sorry, but I still forgive all of my exes. And then I forgive myself.

I call every sleep a baptism.

I remain soft and always wear lipstick. I send out some poems as mating calls. I am shameless. I am romantic. I am wanting, and it is wonderful.

I romanticize every bad date, saga of kissing and ridding demons and trolls and dull princes.

I want to be savagely in love. I want even the wolves to fear the things we do beneath the moon.

I've written about love one million times, but I'll never be an expert on it. No one is, and no one can be. One million different things happened to your heart to turn it into the landscape it is today, as unique as a snowflake. The notion of one formula for handling all hearts is impossible and absurd.

People will keep floating through your life like a river of souls. Some will keep going, some will crawl to the riverbed, make a home there, and decide to stay. Humans, even through our ugliness, are in this world to help each other. We are each other's archaeologists, excavating from one another what we could never dig into and find on our own.

You are the common thread of all your great loves. You are what binds all the romance you've ever experienced.

Forget everyone else. Are you worthy of yourself? Are you someone who could be loved by you?

THE ENTIRE HISTORY OF US

you have awakened an ancient longing in me,
a want before my body was built,
a desire waiting patiently before the birth of my bones.
I have already loved you through
every witch burned at the stake,
every queen hanged by the neck,
every empress with her heart on the line—

I have lived in the light for eons
in anticipation of your eyes.

in each of these lives,
you are both the battle
and the armor.

when you kiss me,
I can taste tar and sand and wine
overflowing from the kingdoms
and country sides
and speakeasies that have already seen us fall together
and then fall apart.

wherever you kissed me then
is now a birthmark on this skin;
your fingers follow them like a timeline.

do you remember?
commandments were written
in fear of our kiss,
empires fell to make room
for what we have become.
I knew you were mine
when you held me and my body became
the vessel through which I could travel in time.

with you I have always existed and will always exist.

so, come to me now.

touch me like we were Gaia's sole intention,
like the whole universe formed just for
the potential of us.

unshackle me from the bind
of these years;
time has nothing on the way you calm
the revolt in me.

so, come to me now,
and let us fix Pangea's fate;
I am so tired of drifting apart.

these hearts of ours could find each other
through centuries
and wars,
across highways,
and from opposite stars.

ten light-years over,
after death,
eyes closed,
and in the dark.

ALPHABET SOUP

I am running out of ways to call you a harvest of
birthday wishes, diary pages, and conversations
with every god I ever once believed in
(The Father and Aphrodite and Seventeen Magazine).

to say that you were what I wanted
before Fate even asked—before body, before time;
that I would beg for this even if it wasn't already mine.

that you can undress me down to the skeleton;
that blood red, true love forgets its own privilege—
it reaches the mantle and dreams of the core.

that dinner is served, but I choose to stay hungry;
that the heart is a mirror bound to reflect
whatever it is turned towards.

that I am lowering myself into the dictionary,
a bucket at a well.

(how many more constellations
can I use to mention your smile?
how many more myths
can I summon to call out your name?)

here is another paper monument, another shrine of words:
you make language restless dreaming beyond itself,
you make twenty-six letters feel like a cage.

TEN QUESTIONS I ASK WHEN I'M FALLING IN LOVE

1. what is love to you: sacrifice or compromise?
2. what's the worst thing you've ever done?
3. what's the best thing you've ever done?
4. what location will you haunt as a ghost?
5. if we had two flight vouchers anywhere in the world, where would we go on our next date?
6. in which past life do you think you got that birthmark?
7. name a star after what you love most.
8. what do you do when no one is looking?
9. is there a book that altered the course of your life?
10. can you touch me from across the room?

DREAMS

being a writer is visionary.
a writer infatuated is clairvoyant.
my heart has its hand on a pen,
always working on my love story
before it's even started.

I keep thinking about my person, somewhere out there. I
keep thinking about rough thumbs on my bottom lip, peaches
and leather, silver thistles and classic horror, drive-ins and
long stretches of road, the whole season burning and things
getting better, better, better.

they admonish me for this,
but when I choose you, I will be certain,
I will be ready,
the starting line will feel familiar,
the air horn will not startle us,
our engines will rev smoothly.

how powerful it is
to invent what you love
before it has the chance to love you.

in my arms
and under my pen,
you will never feel like a trick of the light
or an obligation of fate.
you will see me for the first time
and recognize me right away.

you are the chapter I penned with
my eyes open and hand steady.
I decided on you.
this affection is deliberate.

a soul mate is not a plot twist,
nor shooting star,
nor wishbone.

it is falling to your knees
and opening yourself up to what you invited in,
saying, "welcome home."

JULY

moon
I am moonstruck.
your anatomy must be
constellations for limbs,
carnival lights for eyes,
woodwind lips, teeth like piano keys,
your chin in Michelangelo's hands,
the mountains of your shoulder blades,
your smile at sea.
your inventor assembling you in parts,
hunched over a conveyor belt of my dreams.

big dipper
I think a part of myself
will always exist on that northernmost tip
where you told me you loved me
and the whole sky was descending
upon us and the stars formed to speak
on how I felt in return.

north star
I am both embracing time and running from it.
when things are good, they are spectacular,
but I feel as though I will die if I have to let them go.
love has never been so kind to me,
I am mourning moments as I live them—
and they are somehow reborn
even brighter seconds after.

SEVEN LETTERS TO LUCIFER FROM GOD

i. morning star,
king of Babylon,
what is it that you call yourself now?

ii. perhaps I loved you too softly,
perhaps I should have kissed
more fear onto your tongue.

Peter will read this.
I digress.

iii. by the time I warned you not to play with matches,
you were already on fire.
by the time I tried to knight you,
you were already wearing a crown.

morning star,
when I called you my lionheart,
did you not take it as a compliment?
when I gave you your wings,
did you mistake a gift for an opportunity?

iv. they say that you can only love a king for so long
before you must become one yourself.

how terrible,
that your idea of heaven
could be someone else's hell.

v. I keep writing prayers through the lips
of dying men in case you might hear them.
as we forgive those who
trespass against us.

I keep spitting out meteors
to understand what you felt,
but they barely break the earth.

vi. morning star,
don't tell the angels
that I would trade them all
even
for this singed version of you.

vii. once, we were out smoking on a cloud,
you leaned over and
lit my cigarette with your halo.

I warned,
"careful,
you might fall."

CREATION

do you remember
when there were no countries?
do you remember the earth before
we sank our butter knives into it?

you came to me,
and I was divine.

I love you how a god must love,
building all this just to
give you something to break.

EAST AND WEST

here is a laughter the night cannot swallow,
here is the warmth and soft violence
of light pouring into a dark room.

here is the boy my future will not surrender,
here is the cliff's landing; here is what's true.

I studied the myth and never knew an Atlas
that was begging for my burdens.
(here is the star-map on his back,
here is the scroll of his spine)

here is everything I do as an ode to you:
the way I drink my coffee is the sister
of your mouth on mine.

here is a barter with the fates,
such a cacophony there is only peace.
here is the boy, parkouring the grit of it,
here is the girl he loves ruling
over the space in between.

THE DEFINITION OF LOVE

everything I am afraid of,
you are feeding to me for breakfast.

there are ghosts in the apartment
that howl when you're gone.

for the first time,
I peel back the skin to bite down on the bone.

I don't want to sleep.
I never want to sleep.

someone once told me,
"be careful with a love like this,
the kind that makes you forget
everything and everyone else,"

but I don't remember who.
I can't remember now.

FOUR APOCALYPSES

reincarnation, do your worst

i. we never went to church
so I guess this is what we get,
the locusts lick their lips as you
lick mine and speak to me in rosary beads,
one whisper at a time
and all your sins meeting mine;
the rapture finds
that you've already forgiven me.

ii. you say something awful like,
I can survive this because you were already a storm
category five with a slight chance
of self-destruction;
you keep shouting my name from rooftops like an SOS
I guess
I keep forgetting what I need to be saved from.

iii. the virus spreads, and it's a mania,
feverish and out of control;
you seem to be hungry for what's left of my heart
nothing new there but
do you know the corner where
they're giving out chances because
I've just run out of those.

iv. solar radiation swallows us whole
and looks like the beginning and end of the world;
you tell me we should name our kids sun-kissed,
but when I laugh
I'm also crying.

and so we keep saying things like,

reincarnation do your worst
and
what a curse,
to keep meeting at the end of our story.

TELL HER NOW

tell her now,
while the tea is still boiling,
in the middle of the street,
with the trees leaning over to watch
and the lampposts flickering their eyes in surprise,
her bags packed with all of your second chances.

tell her now,
before the bombs burst,
before Hades gets his hands on what you were,
before Act Two becomes a bloodbath,
before the crown gets its claws in your heart,
before the apple catches her eye,
before she leaves,
before you die.

by the time we see the stars above us,
they have already lived full lives.

somewhere in Italy,
a man cannot decide what to pack for a train
that has already arrived.

tell her now,
if it is the last thing you say,
if it is the last mistake you make.

I would rather be blinded by the sun
than end with my eyes closed;
for it is never too late
until it is too late.

THANK YOU

we sit on the hood of your car,
and I lick the mango juice off your fingertips.
the sun paints us a deep orange;
the gas station shouts its neon right back.

you stand in between my legs with a toothpick
in your mouth, and my dress rides up,
and my thighs are toasted red.
this is the most honest memory I have.

I cut my bottom lip on your family ring
and lick the blood off, too.
my cigarette singes the hem of my dress.

I am the pretty portrait hanging over the mantle
that you've never looked at too closely
until the day that you do.

there is a wheel missing from
the bus trotting down the horizon.
there is a stroke of auburn
where the sky should be blue.

you squint at me,
and my details finally come into focus.
you realize, I am not Helen,
just the war.

but you don't run,
you bare your teeth and brace for impact;
you do not hide it.

you give me what we are all looking for:
someone who loves us because of what we are
and not despite it.

NAISSANCE

"have you ever been in love?"

"yes."

"what did it feel like?"

I think of you,
I think of one night feeling like one thousand.
I think of us with our claws out,
trying to hold hands,
wolves among the apple trees,
mistaking everything for blood.

I think of the fact that I started this poem
three years ago
about somebody else.

I do not know if this makes me romantic or not:

until you,
I couldn't finish it.

ECHO AND NARCISSUS

1. the glass is:
    a. half-empty
    b. half-full
    c. a mirror

2. her eyes were:
    a. honey
    b. dill
    c. a mirror

3. the mirror:
    a. shows you what you are
    b. reminds you of what you are not
    c. all of the above

4. what did you see in her that terrified you?
    a. too much
    b. not enough
    c. yourself

LOVE AS PERFORMANCE

he touched me with too much purpose
nothing of himself reached for me without a stage
I wanted to be loved, not convinced

A POSTSCRIPT FROM JUDAS

I do not want you mildly,
I want you wildly.

I want you mindless,
bodiless.
no coat of armor,
no costume party.

I want you open
and broken.
I will not regret your
sunrise nor set.

I want your skin,
I want your sins.

(how do you love
the wrong way?)

I want my atoms to form lips
that only know your name.

no blood and body,
just ash and flame,

and when they tell your death, lie.
say that I am the one you blame.

AND LIONHEART

there is a quote in The Iliad:
"never bury my bones apart from yours, Achilles,
let them lie together."
I never understood before.

but lately I've been
searching for your eyes in the constellations.
perhaps Andromeda's chains are much like
my salvation,
for I can no longer remember myself
without seeing you.

so Achilles,
take my bones and wear them as your armor
and punish me for your victories
if you need to;
there is fire and there is ruin
but I would rather burn with you
than risk the quiet.

because without you,
the gods are holding their breaths,
the world is quiet here;
everything has changed and
so much of me is simply you.

I guess
I never understood before.

PAPER AND BONES

A note from Ava:

This begins on an airplane.

A lot of stories do. But for us, it was different. It was a testament to who we were, who we never were. Callum and I would never have that first glance at the town's square, or a bent oak tree scarred by our own crooked initials. We were not little children when we met, not in the literal sense, anyway. He did not pull my pigtails, and I was not the girl who lived next door. He was not even the boy in the bookstore, two rows down, hands on my favorite novel.

We were flawed. We never pretended to be anything else.

That being said, I had always wanted to claim a point for us amidst the nothingness that is the Atlantic Ocean, something solid that I could curl into whenever he'd undoubtedly have to leave me. But a magic like that never really was on our side. In the end, all we have is Flight 139 on a discontinued airline, letters that were burnt in the fall, cities that do not remember our footsteps, and memories that are fading.

Memories that could have never happened at all.

All I can tell you now is that I'm carrying all that we have, and it doesn't leave room for much else. I understand the dreadfully wonderful way that life works. You'll meet one person, and you'll adopt their pain, tangle it with your own, steal kisses and quote words like puzzle pieces to a picture that has never been taken. You'll meet one person, but it won't matter if you're sure.

Because this isn't one of those stories. Bells are ringing, and the low hum of violins has never sounded melancholier. I'm wearing white, I'm looking into a reflection through a veil so thick that I cannot recognize myself. And in the other room, down an aisle I never wanted to walk, between a sea of people that were never supposed to witness this flawed decision, there waits a man who loves me.

He's wearing black, and his tie matches the lilacs in my hair.

He isn't Callum.

So no, this isn't one of those stories. I don't even know what kind of story this is.

You'll have to figure that one out on your own.

une

If strangers came with disclaimers, theirs would look like this.

The girl in 17C: Lithe bones, bronze skin, hair like silk's thicker sister, and curves she just recently befriended. Eyes dripping honey. A glutton for dark romances. Speaks incessantly—with a falsetto, with a flourish—of literature, of the dusty dark corners of history, of cobwebs and stage plays, of lipstick and blood, to anyone who will listen. Dresses in costume more often than contemporary. Wants to be a ballerina and also happy. Has a stutter in her want.

The boy in 18D: Call him Icarus. Pale skin and bruised in bad places, starved for the sun. Charcoal fingertips, a battered leather duffel bag, and a thing for watching indie films in dark, cramped theaters—feet on the seat in front, stale popcorn on the tongue. Wears handprints like tattoos of years with cold fingers dug into his shoulders. Comes from old money and new issues—a bad gambling habit and a fist that craved his cheek. Blonde hair cropped short at the sides and rumpled in front, eyes to freeze rather than drown in. A mean punch. A brave heart. A gentle one.

Looking right at her.

————

At first, they existed in glances.

The flight attendant announced something in her staticky voice, and the girl tapped her pen along to the beat of it. Callum's gaze skipped off the cover of his journal as he leaned back in his seat to watch her fidget for a moment.

It was the T-shirt that did him in the moment he scooted by her to shove his duffel into the overhead. It was feathered gray and loose on her, but clung close to her shoulders like she had been its favorite owner. It blared BOTLEY CRUE in jagged red print, a rock band of robots jamming out underneath it.

Callum hadn't realized he had been staring until she crossed her arms over the one with the mullet. Tired travelers were shuffled and shoved by as he glanced up to find that the girl was also staring at the center of his plain white V-neck.

"Seemed fair."

"Fair enough."

They smiled at each other.

It took him a few more seconds to realize that she was with her family, gaze finding the like-faced little brother monkeying around behind her, a woman older than the girl but reminiscent in features narrowing her eyes at what was unfolding.

Callum turned back to the girl and smiled crookedly.

He repeated, "Fair enough."

The eight hours that followed were a careful game of Goldfish. Card for card, look for look. She brushed her chin against her shoulder, eyes brightening when she caught him looking. He ducked his chin, smiled down at the tray before him.

She angled the book in her hands so that he could catch its torn cover— a Tim Burton biography. And he raised his paperback over his face like a mask, allotting her a glance at his edition of *Big Sur*.

She raised a brow, and he nodded his head. And when time zones trickled into each other, they both dozed off for a bit, and their hands fell towards the aisle, fingers twitching like something was just out of reach.

———

Everything in the last leg of the flight seemed better in his company. They wrinkled their noses at the soggy cartons of meat and pasta surprise, and he tossed Ava his fork when she dropped hers on a particularly cruddy piece of carpet. And when some romantic comedy aired on the shared television screen of the plane's divider, they breathed with the same silent laughter, turned to each other at the same jokes.

One look he shot her, dark in the eyes, mischievous in his smile, sent a flush across her skin, guised only by the dark.

Ava was suddenly grateful that she came from a family of deep sleepers.

The spell was only broken when she got up to use the bathroom, stumbling through the aisle. The entire plane was in sleep mode: headphones in, pillows propped up, and *will you get off my shoulder please?* As she passed, she held onto the back of his seat, and he steadied her with a hand on her hip.

Ava parted her lips to say something, but he retreated in a flash.

And when she surfaced from bathroom, he was standing there again, leaning against the plastic partition, waiting to go next. Her heart pounded; a toilet flushed.

Modern day romance.

"Vacant!" she exclaimed in a manic rush, nearly hitting herself for it after.

He ducked his head to conceal a laugh. He made no move to pass; she made no move to return to her seat.

"Good movie," he remarked.

Ava frowned. Perhaps they hadn't been throwing each other the same looks after all.

"Not my favorite."

He leaned in as if he were about to share a secret. "Sarcasm. A seven-letter word…"

Ava smiled. "I'm—"

"Hi, you two," the flight attendant suddenly cooed, sliding in between them. He scowled, stumbled back. Ava let out the breath she'd been holding, ran her fingers through her mussed hair. "We're about to hit some turbulence, so we'd greatly appreciate you returning to your seats."

He parted his lips to say something, but Ava was already nodding, tiptoeing back.

The hour after was much too short, and their glances grew more urgent, more expectant. Ava's mother warned her she'd get whiplash, turning her head around like that, but didn't comment on it further.

And when they touched New York City, they shared the same pained jerk at the landing. He opened his mouth; she bit her lip.

"Bye," he mouthed, reaching for his bag in the overhead.

She exhaled, nodded back, caught on the lines of his back for so long she almost missed the abandoned journal that had taken his place in 18D.

———

from: goodbehava@xmail.com

to: cgray@zmail.fr

Dear Paris,

I don't know when this will get to you. After all, you were heading to New York when you clearly live in France. I hope you have a good vacation—if that's what it is.

This is the girl who played eye tag with you in seat 17C. And I think I have something of yours. Thank goodness for "if found, please reach…" pages. Ha.

Oh, don't worry about the innermost details of your life. I didn't sneak a peek at your book. I have no idea what's in it, and it'll remain that way. I have a journal myself, and I know what it's like…to lose it.

It's like losing your past.

And if you don't have that, where do you even start, right?

You have twenty-four hours to deposit one million dollars into my bank account if you ever want to see this baby again.

Your Friendly Neighborhood Journal-Napper, New York

P.S. Is this weird?

————

"Hey man. It's really great that you're back and all, but your shit has been piling up in the mail bin. Move it."

Callum was barely able to shove the door to his flat open when Thomas, one of his two flat mates, called the weak words out in his usual monotone.

The sound filtered through the rooms, from Thomas's untouchable cave to their third friend Brynn's rat's nest to the hallway Callum was standing in now.

It was Thomas's signature attitude, and not even a week-long stay-cation had loosened him up to a bit of clutter. Callum rolled his eyes and kicked the door closed, dropped his bags so roughly that their superintendent was sure to feel the miniature earthquake three stories down. That was how much of a shithole they lived in. Which was awfully ironic, considering that Thomas's obsession with tidiness had gotten that much worse in the year they'd been rooming together. The ad he'd posted when Callum and Brynn, fresh off the drop-out boat, were first surfing for apartments was quite the understatement.

"Laid back freshman looking to co-own a bachelor pad."

Callum's eyes found the dingy milk crate that Thomas had proclaimed their mail bin. It was filled to capacity with envelopes, magazines, square packages that were neatly tucked away into two rows. The neon sticky note on top of the stack read, "Callum, please remove" in angry red lettering.

Right.

Callum's shoulder bone gave a sharp crack in protest when his other bag, a thick black duffel, slid from it. He dropped the handle of his suitcase along with it and headed over to the crate, hauled it onto their kitchen counter.

Callum sifted through bills, catalogues, and a suspicious envelope announcing that he'd just won

3.5 billion euro in the French jackpot. Yes, he certainly was popular.

He pulled out the orange package sitting at the bottom of the crate, jammed under there thanks to Thomas's undying consideration.

It was from his mother.

It wasn't a care package, wouldn't be filled with his favorite chocolate bars, or a game he could spend hours playing on his Xbox, not like the things Thomas got and proceeded to stash away in his room. Just a half-blank postcard and a plain blue tie.

The thing smelled like Chanel No. 5 and expensive fabric, like everything else he'd known during his short childhood spent in Manhattan before his father had moved them all to Paris, and he wondered which one of his mother's errand boys had been paid off to sneak in the Saks bag this time.

Those scents weren't allowed by the in-home care nurses.

Callum's fingers twitched, fists itching to punch, feet aching to run.

"Can you move—"

Callum knocked the mail bin to the floor, then kicked it over to his room.

"Happy?"

Thomas made an unintelligible noise.

Callum's room was mostly bare. He'd spray-painted a few cartoons on the wall by his window, where most of his belongings were splayed out on the sill.

The air mattress he slept on played house to his computer, which dinged upon his arrival.

He frowned, bent over it, scanned the contents of the email he'd just gotten.

All at once, everything stopped.

His hand halted its shaking, and he smiled.

————

from: cgray@zmail.fr

to: goodbehava@xmail.com

Dear New York,

Was that a ransom note? This is the last time I trust a pretty face.

Thank you for recovering my journal, even if it was through theft. I owe you big time.

So, name it. What's your "big time"?

Your Scorned Victim, Paris

P.S. It doesn't have to be.

————

"Hey sweetheart. Let me talk to you for a minute." The hollers sat and passed like a foul odor, and both girls crinkled their noses. "Damn, Ma," the man continued to his unaffected audience, "I would tear that up."

"Oh, be still my heart," Ava sighed as her best friend Faye lifted her middle finger in the air. "Have more romantic words ever been uttered?" She closed her eyes and spun around, fingers clutching at the fabric over her heart despite Faye's protests. "We're to be married on this very street corner. He had me at *tear it up*."

Ava laughed, her dress billowing out around her thighs as Faye yanked at the crook of her elbow.

"Pursue your death wish when I'm not around, okay?"

"He didn't even hear me."

Faye frowned, slapping a strand of hair away from her lip. "Did you want to go back and rehash it with him over a cup of coffee?"

Ava shrugged one shoulder and grinned. "He had this *way* with words."

"Shut up."

"Sorry," Ava sniffed, chucking an invisible piece of lint at Faye's cheek. "It's just exhausting. What happened to romanticism?"

Faye smirked. "Nudes?"

"Guys standing on balconies with bowler hats on, curtsies and first dances," Ava continued, cheeks tinted pink. "Now, I'm lucky if a guy won't take a winking face as a cue to send me a picture of his *you know*."

Faye nudged her shoulder. "Now *that* is romantic."

Ava pretended to puke. "I'm serious. This generation is so screwed." She lifted her cup of coffee, specks of brown tainting the hem of her gloves as she waved it around. "Here's to you, 2016's Romeo. Where for art my Facebook poke?"

"Nudeth for nudeth?"

As Faye cackled, Ava rolled her eyes, tripped her friend en route up the stairs.

"Hilarious."

Faye made herself at home as Ava rushed over to her computer. The number of times she'd hit refresh earlier that day wasn't one she was proud of.

But as she went to indulge herself in more clicking, she found that there was no need.

Her heart skipped to the sound of quick typing.

———————

(1) Friend Request

Ava Rios is now friends with Callum Gray.

Ava: Hey stranger.

Callum: Where's the lie?

Callum: I'm going to have to see the face of the criminal who's holding my book hostage.

Ava: Sweet with words, I see.

Ava: Okay, Casanova.

Callum: Okay.

Callum: Is this weird?

Ava: It doesn't have to be.

————

The butterflies in Ava's stomach were on a rampage, and Callum was loading on her screen.

Seeing him on camera was different from the slivers she'd caught of him through peripheral glances and shy smiles on the plane. Different from the two profile photos he had up: one of him spraying graffiti on a dirty wall over the Seine, the other of him as a baby, painted over with a mustache and leather jacket.

This Callum was wearing a button-up shirt that didn't quite fit the black ink cityscapes tattooed down his arms, leaking into a swirl of unintelligible patterns down to his knuckles. His hair seemed to have been combed back just a minute before.

He'd been biting his lip before he realized that the camera had connected him to Ava.

"Hey."

Ava waved. "Hi."

On her end, she wore a blue party dress costumed in thick jewelry. The blanket she had with the Eiffel Tower threaded on it hung behind her.

"So that it feels like we're in the same place," she joked.

Callum laughed.

"And," Ava continued, "I like to dress like a madwoman so that there's no confusion about what's underneath."

Callum nodded. "Madness?"

Ava smiled and echoed, "Madness."

"I want to know your madness." He perched closer to the screen, licked his bottom lip. On impulse, she did the same.

"I'll send you a slideshow," she smirked, but there was a trip in her words. "It's nice to *officially* meet you. I'm Ava. And you are…"

"Really happy to see you."

———

In the summer, they sat at their windows, listened to their cities play different songs. She'd convinced him to take paint to paper rather than spray to street, and then spent hours watching his canvases evolve from thick lines to entirely different worlds, portals past the gates of his mind.

She practiced ballet in front of him, and he pretended he knew a single thing about dance. Critiqued her technique, stroking the stubble on his chin until she'd fold into a fit of laughter.

In the fall, they talked endlessly with tired tongues. Two years older than her, Callum was working at some grocery store by day, dance club by night. It turned out that he'd been an heir to old money and a father with a bad temper. His family had lived all over the world, but no travel could change the swing of the man's fist.

His mother had run back to New York and left he and his sister with their father in Paris until he'd abandoned them too. One diagnosis later, Callum was still learning how to forgive her.

Ava had always lived in the city, always would. She seemed to attract people who did a lot of leaving—her father being the first. She carried her heart around in her hands, despite what could happen to it.

She, her mother, and her brother lived in a loft, and she had wide eyes for art and everything it promised. She spoke of NYU, and he'd spend hours with his bleary eyes on bits and pieces of her application as she dreamt of interweaving her love of dance with her love of story, turning old words into new routines.

"Like, hybrid art," Ava explained. "Is that stupid?"

It didn't matter what hour it was on her end or his, Callum's chest never stopped thrumming for the way her eyes lit up at the idea.

"It's brilliant."

In the winter, he bought her holly flowers and set them in front of the computer. She dressed in faux silk, and his fingers itched to touch her. He traced her dimpled smile through the screen.

Ava's eyes sparked with something he couldn't deal with from so far away.

"What do you want?" she asked, and she let the strap of her dress fall off one shoulder.

His fists curled at his sides.

In the spring, she wrote him a love letter that pretended not to be. He took it everywhere with him until Thomas and Brynn got a hold of it.

Then he hid it everywhere with him.

She tried on costumes for him, and he showed her his first finished painting. It was of his mother, what she'd looked like before she'd gotten sick. She wore a designer gown and puppet strings on her limbs. And still, she was running.

Ava cried.

He listened to French rap, and she tapped her feet to instrumental ballads. Both bled heartache to a different beat.

And always, it ended with weak voices and worn smiles.

"See you in a minute," she'd whisper. "Yeah," he'd say, "See you in a minute."

———

"She's just like," Callum sighed, raking his hands through his hair as if the movement would rid her of his constant thoughts. "Like seeing your favorite painting behind glass. It's touched you unlike anything else ever has, but you'll never be able to touch it back."

He stubbed his cigarette out against the stone wall that leaked into the Seine. A few teenagers laughed across the river. A flustered father caught his toddler from wandering too close.

"Fucking poetic, that is," Brynn said.

The two boys were opposite sides of the same dark coin. They'd both been born into excess—Brynn's mother and father were some sort of extended royal line in England, and Callum was an unwilling heir to blood money—and they'd both fled from it.

They had dropped out of the American University to stir up trouble in the city together, two boys itching for something more.

Of course, Brynn was boisterous and brilliant with his music, boom boxes down quiet romantic streets, leaving streaks of color wherever he went.

Callum was a brooder with a sharp tongue, preferred to leave his mark with dark paint on canvas and clung onto hope with the stories that existed *beneath* the streets.

Different brands of the same chaos.

"Fucking surreal," Callum said, lighting another. He pulled the beanie from the mess of blonde on his head again.

"Dude, what fucking plane ticket did you buy? Last flight I took was up to London, and the dude next to me was farting start to finish. Didn't even need gasoline, the engine.

Could've shot us straight across the pond with that flatulence."

"Jesus, man."

Since Callum met Ava, Brynn had been off in London pursuing a potential record deal, recording samples and leaving Callum to fend for himself with Thomas.

Perhaps Ava had pulled the sentimentality out of him as well, but it now dawned on Callum how much he'd missed his friend.

"Just true." Brynn raised his brows. "So, you love her, she's your dream girl. Tell her."

"She doesn't even know me," Callum said. "I don't know her. What am I supposed to say? The glow of the computer screen makes your eyes look beautiful? Oh yeah, and I've fallen in love with you."

"Oh," Brynn replied, mimicking a breathy female voice. "Callum, take me now. Take me *now*."

Callum slapped him across the back of his head. "Hope someone tosses you in the Seine. They don't, I will."

Brynn snorted, stole a smoke. "Wouldn't be the first time." He held up a finger. "Look mate, since you met this girl, you've been painting all the time, haven't been worrying as much about your mother, lookin' at the future like there's something there now. Keeping her to yourself and won't even show me a picture because you're so protective, and you know I'd snatch her up." He paused for effect, and Callum grimaced. "Can't even see your past on your face anymore. That's an *I love you* in so many words." Brynn jabbed at Callum's shoulder. "So what. The fuck. Are you waiting for?"

Legs dangling over the dirty waters below, Callum swore he saw a flash of Ava's smile in the sun across the Seine.

"Yeah," he said, "I don't know."

———

"Okay," Ava called from where she was hanging over her bed, reading from one of those awful sleepover topic games. She wore wide-brimmed orange glasses and a long white gown, her hair a mess tumbling down to the ground.

Callum had his computer down on the kitchen counter, giving her the perfect view of his mayo-spreading technique.

She continued, "Describe your soulmate."

He smirked, "Look in the mirror."

Ava picked a stuffed animal up from near her bedpost and threw it at her webcam. "Take this seriously, Grump."

His hands halted for a second before continuing. "I am."

———

On Ava's eighteenth birthday, she went dancing.

She lost herself in red and blue lights, some black-walled club that didn't fit her pink dress and kitten heels in the slightest. She and Faye waltzed to reggae and skipped to dubstep.

Along for the ride, their friend Lucas watched from the sidelines, eyes on Ava. Always on Ava.

She smiled in tune, pretended that Callum's absence didn't weigh as heavy as a human being. That she didn't keep looking for a face in a crowd that wouldn't be there.

"So, Ava," Lucas asked when they went to get drinks, "I was wondering if maybe I could take you out to dinner. Y'know a birthday dinner or —"

"Oh, Lucas," Ava called back over the music, tucking her hair behind her ear. "I'm actually not available."

Faye added, "She's in love with a computer."

Ava cut her a look. "Faye."

"Oh, come on. You spend more time on that thing than you do talking to anyone in real life. It's unbelievable."

"Why are you being mean about this?"

Faye sighed, "Because you're letting this guy toy with your emotions when he's halfway across the world and could be married with seven kids for all we know." She paused, retracting. "At least establish what the hell you're doing if you're going to waste so much time on him."

Ava swallowed.

Lucas stared at the space between them. "So that's a…no to dinner?"

———

"What are we doing?"

Callum paused his typing, glanced up at where Ava was leaning over her computer screen, eyes narrowed at him, a little tipsy.

He looked away again, amused. "Video chatting."

"No," Ava cut in, "no sarcastic one-liners, no cryptic conversation, no more pouring my heart out and letting myself fall for a boy in a box when I don't even know if I mean that much to him."

She paused, scolded herself for the confession.

"Ava…" Callum let out a breath. "Ava, sit down."

Eyes shut, she sat. "Look, Ava."

She opened one eye again, found him sitting in front of his screen with a lit candle and small cupcake, her name written with icing across it.

"Happy Birthday." He leaned over. "I feel *exactly* the same way." Ava touched the screen over the place where the candle was flickering, made a silent wish as he continued, "Sometimes I wonder if I imagined you. My girl, paper and bones." Callum smiled. "But I don't know if I'm capable of inventing something so perfect."

"Yeah?"

Callum blew out the candle, elbows on his desk. "Yeah."

"If I were there right now," Ava asked, hand still on the screen, "What would we be doing?"

Callum raised a brow. "We're really doing this?" He smiled. "Perv."

She threw a blanket at her camera. "I'm serious."

He hesitated only a moment before whispering, "Why don't we find out?"

————

"So, your girl is coming, eh?"

"Yeah, man," Callum smirked, though it collapsed into a goofy grin. "You'll get to meet her."

On the other end of the line, Brynn made a ruckus of something in the background before agreeing.

"Look man, I'm just saying that if you pull a quick one and make Thomas your best man, I'll kill ya, I will."

Callum chuckled, then paused.

"Hold on. I'm getting another call." He frowned. "That's weird. It's from New York."

————

The red dress seemed silly now amidst the hustle and bustle of the airport. A black curl stuck to Ava's lip as she maneuvered the crowd, an uncomfortable mixture of too slow and much too fast. The natives were in skinny pants, women with hair piled up in sleek buns, men in crisp white

T-shirts, aviator sunglasses buried in well-quaffed hair. And then there were the tourists, loud babbling only matched by the sound of their squeaky white tennis sneakers against the linoleum.

They all looked at her, the bright scarlet, the boisterous curls, like *who does she think she is, Audrey Hepburn?* And through it all, Ava rolled her little case down to the main exit, which she half understood from a blur of arrows and signs dripping with French accent marks. She bit down her flush and—

"Hey, girl. Follow me off the plane, did ya?"

Ava spun around. The Brit who'd been sitting near her on the last leg of her connecting flight making endless corny jokes and conversation—a quality source of entertainment, she wouldn't deny it—was standing before her now, and the gel in his hair had clearly withstood the plane ride in.

She rolled her eyes, steadied herself, then continued on her way—in the opposite direction.

"Oh, come on, mate. You're breaking my heart."

Ava let out a small laugh and waved her cell phone apologetically. "Sorry Casanova, I have to make a call. To my boyfriend."

The Brit clutched his heart but nodded in defeat.

He jotted his number down on the back of an extra customs form and gave her a toothy grin.

"In case he doesn't pick up."

Ava rolled her eyes and crumpled it in her fist.

Sitting down at one of the benches by the revolving doors, she tapped her fingers against her thigh as it rang, rang, rang.

"Ava." Callum said, sounding breathless and strained, and she pretended not to catch the nerves in his voice. "Ava, did you just land? I've been trying you for a while."

"I was on this magical, reception-less contraption called an airplane," Ava joked, hands drumming on her own stomach. Had the waist of this dress always been so *tight*? "Maybe you've heard of it." She paused. "It seems to me, Callum Gray, that you're not here."

Another pause. And then he sighed. "That's because I'm not."

Ava pressed her fingertips to her forehead, her mother and Faye's warnings sounding clearer to her than ever.

"Ava," her mother had said at the airport after a few long battles back at home, eyes so dark there could have been a death in the family. "I can't tell you what to do with your money. The money you worked *very* hard to save up with your afterschool job. Though, that's beside the point. I can't tell you who to waste time on and what to do with your life anymore. But think long and hard about the disappointment you'll feel if that boy lets you down. If that's worth whatever you think you're going to find there."

Ava had looked away then. Her mother seemed to be talking about someone else entirely.

Ava inhaled now, tried, "So what, you're stuck in traffic, or…?"

Callum cleared his throat once, then again. "Ava, I'm not in Paris."

Ava shoved down on the handle of her suitcase to sit on top of it, shoulders hunching in disbelief.

"What?"

"Please, listen. I had to…go. My—"

Click.

Heat spreading underneath her skin, the embarrassment was what propelled her to hang up the phone. As if by wishing it away, she could pretend that he wasn't the only reason she was there.

As if she wasn't the cliché girl in the beautiful red dress, crying in an airport for a boy who wasn't coming.

————

On the other side of the Atlantic, Callum cursed, scrambled to dial her again, his black suit like false armor on his body. It went to voicemail, went to voicemail, went to voicemail, and he left shaken message after shaken message, one word tripping over the next in the rush to explain.

"Callum, son," the priest said, taking the phone from his shaking hands, "are you okay?"

Callum's gaze flickered up. "I'm…fine, Father.

Just sorting a few things out."

The priest nodded, folded Callum's fingers back over the phone.

"We'll be starting the service in just a moment." The man paused, and Callum kept his stare neutral on his yellowed beard. "Your mother visited this church many times near the end, Callum. She'd have been pleased that you could finally see it for yourself."

Callum gave him a terse nod.

"She said she saw you in everything. The marble, the sermons, the little children laughing during Sunday School. You and your sister were truly the loves of her life."

Callum pressed the pad of his thumb to the corner of his eye. "Thanks."

"Yes, thank you, Father," another voice interjected. Celine Gray sidled up to her brother as gently as if she were the wind blowing in. She linked her arm with his and gave him a little squeeze. "We'll be seated in just a moment."

Every family had its vodka, every family had its chaser.

Between the Gray siblings, it was very clear which was which. Years spent dedicated to her English and French lessons had turned Celine into the perfect hybrid—a bright and blonde California girl with a French lilt to her words and a rough cut to her diamonds.

Growing up, Callum bore the brunt of their father's temper, and Celine was no stranger to it. But where life had left him callous, it had left her extra kind. And when she was eighteen and desperate to run off to San Francisco to design clothes and get a taste of the Pacific, he'd helped her.

He'd take care of their ghosts for them. He'd always been good at that.

"How are you, darling?"

Callum exhaled. "She's gone."

Celine nodded, bit her bottom lip.

"They said she went happily," she reasoned. "Peacefully."

Callum clenched his jaw. "None of this is how it's supposed to be."

"Hey," Celine said, trying to pat the tension out of his back. "Where's the rowdy, crazy little kid I used to know? How did that smile become a bruised fist?"

Callum cut a glance at her. "Someone punched it."

Someone loved it.

Celine winced at his words, clung onto his shoulder.

An heir and heiress to a throne of dirt, they filed into the church and said goodbye.

———

(15) Missed Calls, (10) Voice Messages

Ava took another brash swig of her cocktail. Even the gothic lights of Notre Dame seemed to stare down in horror. She slipped her phone back into her purse.

"Gotta say," the Brit from the airport beamed, downing another shot like it was water, then leaning back to stare up at the dying sky, "did not think I'd be getting the pleasure of your company on this trip when you stabbed my heart at de Gaulle."

Ava's smile barely appeared before fading again. "Trip?"

He leaned over, ate a handful of nuts from the table. "Yeah, yeah. Thought I'd be seeing an old friend. Plans changed."

Ava practically snorted. "Don't I know it."

"But you are a fine alt—"

The pain was what convinced her to shut him up, the liquor was what encouraged her to do it with a kiss. She leaned across the table, and it was ugly, void of pleasure. The moment their lips touched, she pulled away again, shot up from the table.

"Love, are you—"

On the taxi ride back to her hotel, the Eiffel Tower sparkled some tears for her. She opened her phone only to shoot off an email with no subject.

"You made me forget about endings. And then you showed me one."

———

Callum: ava i'm back home now

Callum: you've blocked me on just about everything else

Callum: pls just listen

Brynn tossed another flower arrangement onto the living room table, then leaned over Callum by the computer.

"This her?" he asked, a consoling hand on his friend's shoulder. There were no jokes exchanged, no dark quips.

Callum nodded, opened the page to her profile picture, one of her eating a croissant at the Bastille Day festival in New York, no doubt once a tribute to him.

So taken with the expression on her face, he almost missed the paled, horrified one on Brynn's. Looking right at the strange girl who'd kissed him a few nights ago.

Almost.

————

Back in New York, no one said I told you so.

Not out loud, anyway.

In the years to come, Ava would remember that set of days as an endless cry, the sort of cry that took everything out of you and left you feeling like you'd never shed a tear again.

Faye and Lucas watched her with pity, brought offerings in tissue boxes and bakery cast-offs.

Her mother spoke to her like she would a lovelorn child, one who went looking for her father's footsteps in the eyes of other men.

Nothing seemed fair.

The third day back brought a knock on the door. Ava barely lifted her head from the company of soap operas and junk food, just listened to a few muffled voices and her mother's footsteps down the hall.

"Ava, you have a guest," her mother whispered, poking her head in.

"Is it death, finally coming to collect?" Her mother rolled her eyes. "Ava, please."

Her sigh was immature and overly dramatic. She swung her legs off the bed, tied her hair up and straightened her appearance into some form of decency.

A blonde girl wearing diamonds and brown leather greeted her at their small kitchen table, smiling when her mother handed her a cup of warm tea.

Something familiar lived in the girl's features—the highlights in her blonde hair, the shape of her eyes. It was like seeing another painting by a favorite artist.

"Hi," the stranger said, her voice like paper curling at the edges with a French accent, "Ava?"

Ava frowned, suddenly feeling very aware of her disheveled state. "Yeah?"

"I'm Celine," she explained, "I'm Callum's younger sister."

Ava's mother glanced between the two, raising her brow at Ava, searching to find a signal for help. When Ava gave none, just stumbled back against the kitchen counter in slight shock, her mother made herself busy "dusting" the foyer bureau.

"Sorry to show up so unannounced," Celine said, gesturing at the seat opposite her, inviting Ava to sit. "Impulse runs in the family, as you may know."

They traded a nervous smile as Ava sat down.

"My brother will never forgive me for this," Celine murmured, staring down at her finger, habitually tracing the rim of her cup. "But I would have never forgiven myself if I hadn't. I understand that you believe he stood you up, Ava."

Ava stared down at the tabletop. "Because he did."

Celine cleared her throat. "Did Callum ever mention to you that our mother lived in New York?"

Ava's brow furrowed. "Yes, it's where he was going when we first met."

"Well, she did," Celine said gently. Her fingers, bone-thin and pale, shook against the teacup in her hands. She reminded Ava of a porcelain doll—their whole family on a shelf marked fragile. Celine's eyes dimmed when she looked up again. "She passed away, Ava. I don't know what universe collided with ours to make sure that your paths would cross in such a horrible way. But when Cal found out that Mother was nearing the end, he got on the first red-eye. He's a mad man for his family, pretends not to be."

Ava had her face in her hands, whispering, *No.*

"And by the time he got here, she was gone," Celine finished in barely a whisper. "My brother is so many things. Reckless, infuriating, stubborn, *rude.*" She smiled, shook her head. "But he's loyal to the ones he loves. And missing the opportunity to meet you again, it wrecked him almost as badly as our mother's death. Forgive him, Ava. He spent those five days missing you and missing her. I could see it. Anyone could.”

Ava caught a teardrop on her thumb. “God, that’s already done. Is he still—”

“He’s back in Paris,” Celine said, sympathy joining her tone. “There was a very small service, and he decided to thrust himself back into work, take care of a few loose ends our mother had in France. You weren’t returning his calls, so he didn’t know whether to risk being *here* or *there* in case you showed up.”

“I’m such a fool.”

Celine smiled, shook her head. Her hand was cold and light when it fell over Ava’s on the table.

“We’re all fools for each other, Ava,” Celine said. “What are you going to do about it?” She squeezed her hand again. “I’ve got to run. Have my own flight back to California. Don’t tear yourself up too much over this. My brother cares for you immensely, even if his gears are a little broken.” Celine paused. “And I see it in your eyes.”

Ava shook her head, confused. “See what?”

“That you two will be under the same moon again.”

Ava smiled, squeezed her hand back before walking her to the door.

“Celine?”

The blonde turned.

“How did you know where I lived?”

Celine smiled. "A postmarked envelope sticking out of my brother's journal. A letter you sent him, I suppose." She nodded at her once before disappearing around the corner. "Says he carries it with him wherever he goes."

————

Callum picked up on the fourth ring.

Ava didn't wait for him to answer before saying, "Hi."

He let the silence eat at them for a minute before he replied, "Hey."

Ava paused, feeling like she'd just set her hand down on a burning stovetop.

"Callum, I—"

"So," he cut in, "You're okay."

Ava bit her lip. "I'm okay."

His laugh was sharp, a little mean. "Well, great."

"Callum, I know how you must feel…"

"No," he rasped, "I don't think you do." There was a shuffle and another pained sound before he asked, "Were you that heartbroken?"

Ava frowned. She was sitting on her fire escape, legs dangling two stories above the city. Above her, the sky was stretching into bed and fading black.

Down below, someone broke a glass bottle of soda. It sounded exactly like whatever was happening inside of her.

"What's your problem?"

He laughed again, bitter and sharp. "My problem is that of every trick of fate to ever fuck with me, this one has to be the best."

"What do you mean?"

"Fun fact, it was my best friend that you kissed, Ava."

The memory came to her like a ripped film reel: slanted and leaned over a table, Notre Dame casting a glow across her skin, a stranger with a thick accent, and feeling like her arms were flailing at the edge of the world.

Ava swallowed and wanted to deadpan, *You're kidding*, but it didn't seem appropriate. Instead, she stated the obvious. "The Brit."

"Is Brynn."

"Callum—"

"I don't blame you."

"You don't?"

"I would've done worse damage. You were hurt, I was hurt. My mother was dead."

His voice was dead, too. Her mind scrambled for anything that would resurrect it.

"I know. Your sister came to see me. Callum—"

"But maybe that's the point of this, that you and I don't know each other."

"What?"

"This thing between us…it doesn't make sense.

Us toying with each other from across the world, making each other promises that we won't be able to keep. Doesn't make sense. I'm here, you're going to graduate in a few months, make it to NYU. There's no version of this story that ends with us together."

"How could you say that? Just a few weeks ago, we were falling for each other. We were talking about love and—"

"Of course we think we're in love with each other," Callum said, exasperated. "We're strangers. There is nothing more romantic than being a stranger to someone. They don't know you at three AM, they don't know how you got that scar. They just know that it's beautiful, but not what you had to do for it. It's knowing someone that fucks everything up."

Ava braced herself on an iron pole, shut her eyes. "That's how you feel?"

His silence was an answer enough.

"Then I agree. You and I don't know each other at all," she said. "Bye, Callum."

Guilt crept up into Callum's throat.

"See you in a minute." It was an impulse, a chipped nail, a bad habit.

"Bye," she said again.

That night, Paris crawled over to the coastline, fingernails in dirt, and cried out to New York, "I'm so sorry about the things I've done for love."

interlude

"Today is terrible, and Pluto is still suffering."

Faye rolled her head back, let out a torturous sigh. "I can't wait until you drop that phrase."

"Faye," Ava deadpanned, waving her pencil like a stubby wand before landing it on her friend's nose, "I, too, am a desolate dwarf planet who was dumped by the solar system."

Faye ordered them three cups of coffee at their favorite place on Third, all wood and steam, vines creeping up the walls and dangling plastic coffee beans. Lucas trailed them, shaking a few packets of sugar like maracas in his palms.

Ava continued, "I, too, am an abandoned shell of light, destined to—"

"Oh, Jesus."

"This has nothing to do with religion."

Faye was still massaging her temples when they grabbed their cups and filed to the garden out back, walled in by four other brown buildings, casting odd shapes of shadow and light in the makeshift yard.

Places like these in New York, the ones that tried to be suburbs, were Ava's favorite. Like dandelions dug from grit and picket fences carved from bone. She dropped down onto a wicker chair, threw her legs over Lucas's lap, and toyed with Faye's hair. "I, too—"

Faye threw a coffee stirrer at her.

Ava smirked, patting down the pleats of her scarlet sundress, then pulling the loose curls away from the back of her neck.

"Whatever, Neptune."

Her laughter was cut short only by Lucas's hand, which cupped her calf as he casually sipped his coffee. Ava shifted uncomfortably, exchanged a glance with Faye.

An entire two years after graduation had done nothing to mar their trio. In fact, they clung and orbited each other more often than ever to survive being thrust into the familiar strange of city colleges and commuter campuses. Faye was a psych major at Barnard, Lucas was undecided at Fordham, and Ava was drowning in the arts—pirouettes danced to the gothics.

But Ivy Joe's was the one corner of the city, tucked behind SoHo, that time couldn't touch.

"Tonight?" Faye mentioned, raising her cup in a false toast. "Are we suffering through Lucas's flannel friends or crashing at my dorm with cold pizza?"

"Your support overwhelms me," Lucas mumbled, squeezing Ava's leg as he adjusted in the chair. He picked up a fallen plastic flower and offered it to her.

Ava smiled, skipped over his gaze.

Faye held a finger up. "Honesty is my only policy Luke-Ass. We love you, but another hour dissecting the origins of craft beer might kill us." Before Lucas had a chance to retort, Faye cut him off with another raised finger and turned to Ava. "You told me to remind you to pick up that edition of *Lolita* for class."

Ava perked up and slid her legs from Lucas's lap to plant a kiss on Faye's cheek. "Life-saver."

Lucas's shoulders dropped, dejected. "Want me to come with?"

Ava shook her head, handed over the cup. "Guard my coffee? It's just down the block." She nudged his shoulder. "Besides, I don't want to interrupt the banter, Abbott and Costello."

With a flounce of her skirt, she was gone, and Faye shot Lucas a sympathetic smile.

She reached over and clinked her cup with his. "Cheer up, lover boy. Your tongue is showing."

Down the block, Ava had her beaten pleather jacket tied like a belt around her waist. The weather was unusually nice for February, a written invitation for Lower Manhattan to haul out the bikini tops, snapbacks, and beer crates. A toddler licked gelato from his fingers, a lost boy played the drums with a can of soup on his stoop. Ava gave him a dollar and a smile before stepping into a corner bookshop.

The place was cold and smelled like freshly printed paper, a combination that made her shiver. She shrugged her jacket on like a shawl over her shoulders and trailed her finger along the hardcovers in Horror.

Bookstores were just shelved cemeteries of bound ghosts. There was not a place in the world she felt more at home.

Her finger was halted by a strange thought, one she hadn't had in months. *Perhaps there was one place in the world.*

"Nabokov, Nabokov, Nabokov," Ava sang under her breath as she stumbled through the aisles. The place was nothing more than a shadow, a dimly lit labyrinth built for customers to discover rather than find.

Frustrated and still mumbling, Ava rounded a corner towards the back, reading the synopsis of a contemporary while still half-scanning the shelves for her pick.

"Excuse me."

(Somewhere, over another ocean: *This is your captain speaking. Prepare for landing. Brace for impact.*)

Ava glanced up momentarily, shifting over so that the stranger could get by, then glanced again.

Her heart stuttered to a near stop. "You."

Callum blinked back at her, hand hovering over her left arm. He parted his lips and made a choked sound, like the letters of her name had forgotten their purpose at the back of his throat.

She inhaled. "Callum."

He let his hand brush her side before it dropped. "Ava."

"You're in New York," Ava stated dumbly.

"Apparently," he rasped, eyes raking over every spot on her face.

Long distance, Callum had been a lightning bolt on the other side of a sea, passing thunder waiting for day to come. In person, he was a storm. Under the dimness of the shop, his eyes darkened indigo. He stood a good foot taller than her, and his hair was buzzed closed to the sides of his head, blonde waves swept back in a style he'd once been too boyish for. He smelled like wood chips and light cologne. Like a renovation, like a new home.

The pace of Ava's heartbeat picked up, reminded her it was still there.

"Hi," she said suddenly, the sharp, unnatural sound startling them both, and reached up to pull him into a hug. Callum's hand twitched midair before finding the center of her back, the mess of her curls. She shut her eyes against his unbuttoned dress shirt, and he held her there for a moment, thumb catching on the bridge of her ear.

"Hey," he whispered against it.

They hadn't realized how long they had been standing there until the bookseller shot them a pointed look over his glasses, clearing his throat as he passed by.

They extricated themselves from each other, and Callum lamely picked up a random book for show.

Karma Sutra for Beginners.

He tossed it aside, scratched the back of his neck with a shy, anxious grin on his face. "Fuck."

Ava pursed her lips, glanced down at the book. "Well, that'll show you how."

Their laughter rumbled the shop. Ava curled into herself, hair brushing his chest as she bent and clutched at her belly. Callum braced himself on a shelf for support, throat hoarse from chuckling so hard. It was a dam bursting, a radio blaring, a beautiful song. A finally, finally, *finally.*

And when there was nothing else left, they stood there, still leaned towards each other, trying to catch their breaths.

Ava straightened first, very aware that he was only a breath away. "It's really good to see you."

Callum cleared his throat, and she watched the jut of his jaw, the dark circles under his eyes, a cut near the stubble on his chin.

He said, "It's really good to be where you are."

Ava nodded. A leather spine pressed into her real one.

———

"I was going to look you up before I got here. Maybe send you a message," Callum admitted as they fell into step on the concrete. Under the sun, he peeled his dress shirt off to reveal the T-shirt beneath, anything to keep him busy enough to not look at her too long.

Last time they'd been standing this close, it had been on a plane, and he hadn't known how much it would hurt him later.

Ava glanced at him. "Yeah?"

He nodded, jaw clenching. "I decided not to."

When he chanced a look at her, he instantly regretted it. She was a blur of color: browns and reds and olives. His gaze caught on every inch of her habits, collecting them to make up for two years lost. She tucked her hair behind her ear, bounced off her right foot with every step, hummed under her breath when she was nervous.

Ava was humming now.

"Not that...I didn't want to see you," Callum corrected, angling himself towards her as they stepped into some earthy coffee shop spilling faded jean hipsters and a trellis of potted plants. He eyed the place cautiously while Ava waltzed in as if she were coming home. "After everything that happened..."

Ava nodded. "I get it." She looked like she wanted to say more, but she was cut off by a terse voice, a girl and boy making a beeline for them from some outdoor space in the back.

"Next time you want to give me cardiac arrest, do it locally," the girl scolded, not even noticing Callum as she curled around Ava like a mother hen. The boy, however, couldn't take his eyes off Callum. There was a slant in his glare and square in his shoulders that seemed a little too much like a threat.

Callum narrowed his eyes at both of them.

Ava smiled half-heartedly. "Sorry, Mom." She glanced at him over her shoulder, and his lips tugged at their corners. "Callum, these are my best friends, Faye and Lucas. Guys, this is…" She inhaled. "Callum."

Faye froze. Looked at Callum, then at Ava, then back at Callum. "I'm sorry, did I miss this on the calendar?"

"Must have," Lucas echoed, eyeing Callum in disbelief.

Faye cleared her throat again and outstretched her hand, still not smiling. "So, you're Paris."

"Yeah, it's on the birth certificate and everything," Callum remarked under a sharp chuckle, reaching out to shake it. "Nice to…finally meet you, too."

Ava ducked her head and laughed through her nose. A child tipped a cup of water over across the room, a fly made its first spring appearance by the light bulb. Callum clenched and unclenched his fist.

And then he set his hand on her back. "Do you want to take a walk?"

"Yeah," Ava replied. "Yes. Sure." She turned to Faye, setting her hands on either one of the girl's shoulders, who was still throwing reluctant looks at Callum. She promised, "I am just a text message away."

"Or a milk carton," Faye sighed, pulling her in for a hug. "Send me messages on the hour. And quit seeing the world so pink." The last statement was pointed at Callum, who stuck his hands in his front pockets, pretended not to hear. "Because it isn't."

Lucas, who'd been oddly quiet behind them, seemed to have found a switch that brought him back to life, a wired smile on his face.

"You're missing out on guitar strumming and kale," Lucas joked, holding onto Ava's arm a second too long to escape Callum's notice.

"Somehow I'll manage," Ava whispered back, touching her nose to his.

Callum's cupped his own jaw, looked away. Ava bit her lip. "Ready?"

"For a while now."

———

The weather cooperated, but New York was on fire because of it, people spilling out onto the streets in masses. They'd made it up to Washington Square Park and trailed a quiet path through the East Village, littering the city with their conversation.

"This is *supposed* to be the part in which some sidewalk singer starts playing a love song," Ava joked as some guy popped a wheelie, then threw up all over his skateboard, much to the enjoyment of his friends. "But it's New York, so I'll take what I can get."

"I don't know," Callum said, thrumming his fingers along to the sounds of the guy retching. "I could slow dance to this any day."

Ava shoved his shoulder.

They stopped at a bar next to a Blues club, and he ordered them a round of beers and dollar slices of pizza.

There was a pause.

"Callum, what are you doing here?"

He swallowed down a gulp of beer. "Archiving the things in my mother's townhouse. Celine and I are renting it out for some extra money, and she couldn't make it up here for the packing." He flicked the rim of the bottle, and it made a little tune. "And I, um, I'm showing at a gallery here."

Ava dropped the slice in her hand onto her plate. "*Hey*, hot-shot."

Callum smirked. "Alright, alright. It's just this hole in the wall on the Lower East Side. Nothing big. A buddy of mine just opened his place up to the public and thought if I was going to be here already…" He ducked his head like a shy kid presenting in class for the first time. "I had every reason to be here." A pause. "I was running out of reasons not to be."

Ava smiled from behind the rim of her bottle. "How long?"

Callum straightened. "A week. Headed home on Friday."

The smile faltered.

When it returned, it was plastered and strained. "God, are you really the same grumpy old man who used to call me on Skype, splattered in paint and bruises?" She rolled her eyes, remembering that wild, dark look in his eyes when

Paris had been his canvas, and he'd refuse to call his dreams by their names.

She added, with a hand over his knuckles, "I'm so proud of you."

Callum nodded slowly, turned his palm up towards hers.

"Always have been."

Ava echoed, "Always have been."

————

If there was any ice to break, the job had been done. They ordered drinks and leaned into each other like, yet again, there's was a game of cards, trading words and old stories, trying to come up with some version of reality in which whatever had happened between them could coexist with the truth.

Ava told him about her sleepless nights, about her double major, and when her eyes lit up describing the way she'd done a ballet installation to Edgar Allen Poe's *The Raven*, all feathers and rustled pages, spinning in the dark, Callum had to brace himself against the bar.

She was the only goddamn person in the world who could take him flying without feet.

"You thought I was weird," Ava suddenly accused him, and Callum realized that he'd lost track of the conversation in his little reverie.

"I did," Callum admitted with a laugh. He touched a curl where it hit her collarbone. "But I liked your weird. You were like a little spitfire. Still are."

"And you were stone," she remarked.

"Still am."

Ava narrowed her eyes, studied him for a moment as if she were a doctor, looking over healing wounds. His edges were still sharp, she still handled him like a child would a drawer of knives, scared to cut her fingers on him. But he was softer in the eyes, his smile came easier. She wondered how many strokes it had taken to paint over his demons.

"No," Ava replied simply, smiling at the bartender for another round.

The guy nodded and made eyes at her, and Callum cut him a look, wrapped an arm around her waist.

Pinned to the wall, beside an ad for a strip club and a poster for The Kooks, was a postcard from Rome. A modern woman waved from the top of an old empire.

It read, "What relief can come from ruin."

———

"Okay, we're going to go see a play. Something dark and Shakespearean," Ava slurred, clinging onto Callum's arm as they stumbled through the streets. He laughed openly as she performed to a lamppost, murmuring something about Hamlet's bones and Juliet's blood. He steered her away from it with an arm slung around her shoulders.

They'd had about the same amount to drink, but he was nowhere near as far gone as she was. Still, a buzz crept up his skin, light bursting from the cracks of him.

"Where are we going to go see this play?"

Ava frowned. "It's New York City. We'll go to Times Square."

"It's three AM."

She sidled up to him at a corner where the broken streetlight was flickering *stop, go, stop, go.*

"Well look at that," Ava replied, hands on his chest, then his shoulders. "I finally know you at three AM."

There it was.

The night had been a skilled game of Chicken—how close each of them could broach the subject of what happened two years ago. Thus far, there hadn't been any spilled venom. But now, she was folding up his cruel words into a paper crane and handing them right back to him.

"We have to do everything right now," she said tiredly, attempting to focus on the moment, "because something bad is going to happen again."

Callum was breathing heavy, and Ava seemed to sober up a bit at the admission. His hand slid up to her arm, to hold her hand over where it was set on his shoulder.

Finally, he asked, "Where's home?"

One heel skidding against the concrete, Ava's smile didn't quite reach her eyes.

Not when she took his hand.

Not when she pointed to the center of his chest.

———

The next morning, she opened her eyes to stark white.

Ava groaned, hid her face under a blur of sheets and mussed-up hair. She was still wearing her clothes from the day before, her legs were tangled up in a foreign comforter, and a gray sweater that didn't belong to her was now wrapped around her shoulders.

The place echoed her footsteps like a museum's halls would. And truthfully, it was worthy of the title. The walls stretched and stood adorned by gilded marble and polished wood. The room she was in was painted a shade of ivory, golden lilies carved into the finishes. Even the nightstand beside her was luxurious, gold-plated and rounded in shape. Her cell phone and purse seemed to litter it. *Unworthy.*

Ava collected her stash and slipped through the door, spilling out into a hallway where the furniture that lined the walls was covered in white sheets, some piled near the grand staircase. She felt small, like another old ghost.

Downstairs, she found Callum staring up at a slanted chandelier in the grand living room, taking steps backwards and forwards underneath it. His clothes were dark, as were his eyes. Ava watched him for a moment before clearing her throat.

"Hi."

Callum halted his steps and turned to her, embarrassed. "Hey." He stepped backwards and reached for a coffee cup and box of scones on top of a taped packing box. "Hope you don't mind that I stuck you in my sister's old room. You insisted on not telling me where your dorm room was."

Ava flushed and shrugged one shoulder. "Peace offering?"

Callum smiled. "Sure."

She sat on the bottom step of the grand stairwell, and he crawled over to join her, his back against her leg. They sipped coffee and nibbled scones in silence for a moment, and she eyed the way the dim light filtering in through the drawn curtains was sparking the scar by his jaw like a white lightning bolt.

"What were you doing under the chandelier?"

Callum turned to her. "Our home in France had one just like this. Creepy almost, how much of a replica this place is. My mother would wake me up at three AM and dress me up in a full suit and tie." He shook his head. "I was six. And she'd make me waltz with her underneath it for hours. I thought it was hilarious."

He downed another gulp of coffee.

"And then one day, my father pressed this switch in her. Just knocked the light from her eyes. And she stopped waking me up to dance underneath it. She'd do it herself for hours and hours until her feet were bleeding, and that's how I'd find her in the morning for breakfast. And I knew then that nothing about life was very funny at all."

"Callum —"

"I'm good," he said, busying himself with crumpling the box and grabbing her now-empty cup. "Are you still hungry? There's not much here, but—"

"Callum."

"And if you need clothes or anything…"

"Callum, I'm sorry," Ava said under a ragged breath. Tears spilled of their own accord as she stepped down from the staircase, faced his curved back, tense in the shoulders. "I should have been there. I should have given this the chance that it deserved. I shouldn't have gone kissing…"

Callum drew in a breath.

"I should have brought flowers to your mother's funeral," Ava said. "I should have been there to hold your hand. I should have come back."

"I'm the one who had to live with letting you go," Callum replied. "I'm the one who had to lie and say that you and I were strangers when no one in the world knows me better. You think that hasn't eaten at me for two years?" He turned around to look at her. "You think someone can go back to loving other people after that?"

Ava shook her head. "No."

"No," Callum echoed. "It should have been us at the Louvre, getting lost in the eras."

She took a step towards him. "It should have been us on the Seine, dancing at midnight."

"It should have happened like this," Callum said, bringing a calloused palm to her cheek, then sliding a few rough fingers into her hair.

Ava exhaled, and they shared the same breath. "Like what?"

And then he kissed her slow. Two year's worth.

———

"You're not really here," Ava whispered a few hours later, lips fallen open against his shoulder. He reached back to skim his knuckle against her cheekbone, up the bridge of her nose, then to smooth out the crease in her forehead.

"No?" he asked. "Do I feel like a phantom?"

She smiled. "Sometimes." She traced the raised skin by his spine, a blistered scar, then the bone of his collar. "You feel like a painting."

Callum turned around to kiss the hollow of her throat. "You feel like a canvas." He held her hand, then pressed it back against the hardwood.

Her eyes fluttered shut when he settled between her legs, and she whispered, "And how do you feel *about* me?"

He pinned her other hand up when her teeth found skin.

"Under the definition of love, you'll always be my 'see also.'"

———

She wore a black gown to the gallery opening, despite Callum's insistence that the place did not call for it. It was on the side street of a side street, had a rickety chalkboard sign out front, and its guests were in denim jackets, sipping wine from plastic cups.

Ava looked more like one of the installations.

Callum kept his hand on her lower back and introduced her as his—no title, no hesitation. Just his.

And then he showed her to a cluster of paintings on a far wall, bristles and strokes she recognized from hours spent memorizing his hands and brushes moving like a dance in the dark through a computer screen.

Callum had transformed famous cities, rebuilt them in scenes filled with marble and rain. There was a dark cloud inside of his version of Versailles, and it rained on the heads of ghost kings and queens. New York City was a hurricane of sea-soaked streets and tenants swinging their legs over windowsills.

Enraptured, Ava's finger reached up to nearly touch one until Callum stole it away.

"Self Portrait" made her cry, for it was a picture of him but not—his face cracked open like a broken globe spilling diamonds and porcelain tea cups and gasoline instead of blood. Scars at the price of riches, and how it had torn him apart.

"You're brilliant," she told him.

Callum gave no response, just took her arms and turned her to a piece she hadn't yet noticed.

The description card simply read, "Ava."

On some night she must have fallen asleep in front of her computer screen, Callum had sketched her as she was, then painted over it with world maps and state lines and miles and miles apart.

There, Point Zero gilded gold on the nape of her neck. There, the Empire State Building standing tall along her spine. The stars over their sea freckled her nose and cheeks. The Atlantic washed over the tendrils of her hair.

Their distance, their story.

As Callum turned to talk to a buyer, another joined the space beside Ava.

"Beautiful work," she said without catching Ava's face.

"Yeah," Ava whispered.

"It's almost like he painted her real enough so that she could step off the canvas. Be with him."

Ava nodded, glanced back at Callum. "Almost."

———

At the airport, Callum couldn't look at her.

"You're breaking my heart," he rasped, tapping his boarding ticket against his thigh. They'd spent every second of the past week together. His mind had known her by heart for a long time, but now his hands did, too. Bookstore visits, outdoor picnics, packing boxes, tangled in sheets and with their words, and more things that were too much and not nearly enough to make up for the time they'd lost.

Ava wiped another tear from her cheek. "Well, just to settle the score."

"This isn't where we're going to end, Ava," Callum promised her, "everything starts now."

Ava smiled, still crying. "Is that what you're going to write in my yearbook?"

He cracked a smile, tickled her side. "I'm the romantic, and you're the wise guy, huh? How the times have changed."

She pressed her forehead to his. "How they have."

"I'll, uh," Callum breathed against her lips, cupping the back of her neck with his eyes clenched shut. "I'll see you in a minute."

Ava nodded. "Yeah, I'll be right there."

Callum hid his face from her, just kissed her once and hiked his duffel bag onto one shoulder, gripping her arm before finally letting go.

"Wait," Ava called, reaching into her purse and surfacing with a journal, his journal, still untouched from when he'd first dropped it. "I can finally give it to you in person."

Callum didn't take it from her, only smiled, walking backwards, raising his clocked wrist. "That's my flight. Guess I'll just have to see you again."

Ava smiled back, clutched it to her chest as he disappeared into the airport crowd.

A phantom indeed.

deux

(10) Missed Calls, (5) Voice Messages (15) Missed Video Calls

ava.rios@xmail.com: Hey handsome! I'm over here making magic with my feet onstage and miss you dearly. Give me a call when—

grayxcallum@zmail.fr: Hey baby. Happy graduation. For the hundredth time, apologizing for not being able to score those tickets. I wish I had the cash. Let me know if you still want to web—

(6) Missed Calls, (2) Voice Messages (10) Missed Video Calls

ava.rios@xmail.com: Hey you. Great news about the company. They're thinking about picking up some of the work I did in college. The Poe piece. Can you—

grayxcallum@zmail.fr: Seeing you for Christmas was amazing. Thanks for making it here. I'm sorry that I couldn't give you a big family to spend it with. Was everything okay—

(3) Missed Calls, (1) Voice Message (1) Missed Video Call

ava.rios@xmail.com: Are you around?

grayxcallum@zmail.fr: Call me back.

No Missed Calls

Callum drummed his fingers against his desktop in a dizzying beat as he waited for Ava to call in.

Around him, the apartment he'd once shared with Thomas and Brynn beckoned for a new presence—the walls were bare save for a few of his more personal art pieces, a set of film tickets, and a stack of books lining the floor.

He clenched his jaw.

Time told the story better than he ever could.

"Hello?" Ava's face materialized onscreen, and he tried to smile. Five years had not touched an inch of her. Her hair was longer, down to her waist, and she wore red lipstick. But her eyes were still young, the song that came from her every word was still singing. He traced the shape of her chin on the screen.

"Hey."

She smiled. "You look good."

Five years had left them closer, then farther apart.

She was working at a dance company that had taken to her multimedia performances. And he had made the slightest of dents in the art scene with his pieces, sold everywhere from street corners to the walls of tattoo shops, while he helped run a restaurant movie theatre in the next district.

Distance found no place for itself in their endeavors, and they'd grown to exist only in missed calls, reaching for phones in the dark, short visits with expiration dates always looming, empty promises, and disappointment.

Callum forced another smile. "You look better."

Ava leaned over and yawned. "I have to run in a few minutes."

He swallowed the sting. "Yeah? Can't stand my face?"

She laughed. "You got me. There's just this cast party for our upcoming production. Lucas—"

"There's a surprise."

"I don't know what your problem is with him. He's played a huge role in my success. That should make you happy. Proud."

"Hey, I've *always* been proud of you. But the stunning coincidence of What's His Face managing a performing arts company that just so happened to pick up your show doesn't escape me."

Ava recoiled. "So, this has nothing to do with my talent, right? I got nowhere without Lucas's high school crush on me?"

Callum sighed. "That's not what I'm saying."

"He's my friend," Ava snapped. "Who is *here*, supporting me. Here."

"Say it one more time," Callum retorted. "Didn't hear you."

"Mature."

"Look, I'm sorry that I can't magically become an overnight sensation and make enough cash to fly in and out like you do. I'm sorry that my art—"

"This has nothing to do with your art. If you had used the money from your inheritance—"

"I want nothing to do with that money, and you know that, Ava. Not until I can make something out of what I have already. You used to believe in that."

"Until you chose proving a point over being with me."

There was a long pause. She turned away from the screen, he put his face in his hands.

"What are you holding onto over there, Callum?" Ava finally asked, facing the wall. "Because it isn't me."

"Don't do that," Callum said. "Don't act like I'm not trying to make this work just as hard as you are. Don't act like I wouldn't trade the world to be with you. Don't act like I haven't lost nights reading every single version of our story, hoping one of them ends with you and I."

"Then what," Ava asked, "are you waiting for?"

"Oh, so I'll come to New York?"

"Why not?"

"Because there is no room for me in your life, Ava," Callum spat. "Because you are moving up, and I am stagnant, and we both know how quickly this is going to fall apart if I move over there with a few paintings and not a dollar to my name. *My* name. Not my parents'. I am fucking walking on eggshells trying to keep you in my life—anyway I can."

"So, don't," Ava said, voice breaking. "Don't anymore."

Callum glanced up at her. She was still looking at the wall.

"What?"

"We're ruining each other," Ava said simply, quietly. "And I would rather let you go than be the one to ruin you."

"Ava—"

"Stop reading," she said, her voice breaking into a sob. "There *is* no version that ends with you and I." On her end, the screen went black. "Callum?"

"Must be the shitty service," Callum said. The "disable camera" window glared back at him on his screen.

Ava drew in a breath, and he could still see her, hands on the computer, like she was trying to reach inside.

"I didn't mean that," she admitted. "You have to go, right?"

"Callum—"

"So do I."

Ava's head dropped. "See you in a minute, right?"

Callum hesitated.

And then he ended the call.

On the next day, her birthday, Callum raised a solitary candle dug into a cupcake to his lips and blew it out.

The computer screen was still dark.

————

Dating Lucas was like trying to sprout roses with dandelion seeds. The growth was there, but nothing would be blossoming red.

Ava said yes to him in the summer after she and Callum stopped pretending they weren't giving up on each other. They rode bikes and laughed over things that friends did and moved into a studio that was all sunshine and wood.

Lucas always called her by her first name, and her spine always rejected his touch, still hung up on Callum's fingerprints.

Her mother loved him; he was always home for dinner.

Her heart called her on the phone sometimes, from someplace else.

————

When the girl who worked cashier in their theater looked at him a little too long to be friendly, Callum swallowed down Ava's name and decided to ask her out.

Marie was from the French countryside and spoke slanted English and always kept her lips stained red.

When Callum kissed her, it was like listening to Bach when he'd asked for Beethoven.

A masterpiece, just not his.

His lips knew the drill, but his heart panged in protest. Angry, it stamped a postcard to Ava.

"Wish you were here."

———

Ava: What's she like?

Callum: I'm not talking about this with you.

Ava: Why? We're friends, right? Is there a problem?

Callum: Smart.

Ava: Great.

Callum: Pretty.

Ava: Expected.

Callum: Fun. Outgoing. French. What the fuck do you want me to say, Ava? That she's not you? That I'd rather be with you? That you haunt me through everything else I decide to love? What can I say that you don't already know?

Ava: Callum…

Callum: Why, what's he like?

Callum: What's he like, Ava?

————

The moon over the fourteenth arrondisement held a peculiar sort of magic—sprinkled like dust across pastel rooftops and pink lights. And from the nightstand by his balconied window, Callum's cellphone howled at it.

He startled out of a dark, dreamless slumber and groaned as the thing blared and chimed. Groggy and blurry-eyed, he caught only the telltale jut of the letters in Ava's name—and the photo of her coy smile, the pattern of freckles on her face, her amber eyes.

Callum sat up, thumb hovering over the button for a moment before answering.

"Hey you."

There was a long, raspy intake of breath on the other side, and Callum pulled the phone away from his ear for a second to double check that the source of the call hadn't just been wishful thinking.

Still Ava.

"So, you're the one."

It was a man's voice that greeted him, dark and irritated, a familiar sort of resentment that he couldn't quite place.

"You're going to ruin her life, you understand? Everywhere she goes, you're with her. Everywhere she goes, she runs into you."

"Who the hell is this?"

"This is Lucas."

Callum swiped a palm over his face. "Jesus, man. Ava and I are friends. Friends who live thousands of miles apart. Can't get any more platonic than the fucking Atlantic Ocean." He glanced at his alarm clock. "Do you know what time it is here? Or what her bill is going to look like when—"

Lucas cut him off. "I'm not an idiot. How does that lie taste?"

It tasted horrible.

"Look," Lucas continued. "If you loved her the way I do, you'd let her go. It isn't romantic. You're always just going to feel like something she failed. Have some decency, give her closure."

Callum bit his tongue, pulling the phone away from his ear. *I don't love her the way you do. I love her something terrible.*

"If you were that worried about this, you'd be talking to your girlfriend," Callum finally said. "Not me."

"Fiancé," Lucas corrected after a long beat. "Think about what I said."

Click.

Callum sent his phone flying across the room, and it brightened before buzzing dead.

The next morning, when he met up for coffee with Marie and told her how he still felt about Ava, she thanked him.

"Now I finally know the name of the girl who lives in your eyes."

————

"You're really doing this now, Faye?"

Ava glared up at her best friend as she clasped a set of dangling black jewels to her ears, a sharp contrast against her pale white gown. It was barely a dress, barely a sheet. It fit like a ghost clinging to her curves.

Faye tied a puff of her curls on top of her head. "I'm just having a conversation with you. Look, I've always loved Lucas in the way you love that one sweet cousin during the holidays. We've always been a triad, but *you and I* were friends. He was just in love with you. Unrequited love."

"Faye, stop it."

"But now, in a rush to get over Paris—"

"Callum."

"You're accepting a proposal that you know in your heart you don't want to accept. I mean, just look at the piece you're about to perform. Where is your head?" Faye paused. "Where is your heart?"

"So what? You want me to go to France? Break him up with his girlfriend? Be with him?"

"I want you to choose what's right for you."

"Yeah," Ava scoffed, "so long as it's what you think is right for me."

Exasperated, Faye caught sight of the leather book Ava was using to balance her makeup tubes. She let out a small noise of disbelief.

"You've been chasing that book for ten years, Ava. And what the has it gotten you?"

"Love," she said, an impulse, a mistake. She winced against the confession, then corrected, "with Lucas. Who is *right* for me. Now I have to go on and perform this piece. I'd really love it if you could at least support me in that."

As Ava stepped out and through a stage door, Faye paused to find her phone before she followed. In the dark of the audience, she hesitated before pulling the device out and lowering the brightness on the screen, thumbs shaking as they searched for a name in the contact list.

She video dialed Callum, who picked up on the first ring. No hesitation.

Another noise of disbelief.

He squinted at the phone in the dark of his apartment, whispered, "Faye? Is that—"

"Just shut up," Faye whispered back, raising the phone as high as she could without giving herself away to the neighboring seats. She turned the camera towards the stage.

The curtains opened, the music played. And then Ava began to dance.

The set was an elaborate hybrid, a metallic reimagining of Paris meeting New York. Garden apartments, open balconies, and flower shops leaked into concrete, skyscrapers and whirring trains from the Seine into the Hudson. And behind it all, the Eiffel Tower leaned towards the Empire State Building, iron hands reaching out to each other from the structures. Just barely touching.

When the music paused for a moment, Faye heard Callum let out a noise.

Aptly titled "A Dance of Two Cities," Ava painted the distance with every thrust and turn of her body, beginning through careful steps, spinning back and forth, then meeting herself in the middle for a sensuous drop to the floor, a pull from the heavens on her torso.

And then it transitioned into something hectic, broken steps, hands in her hair, an invisible storm pulling her this way and back. The crowd held a collective breath when she flipped backwards over an iron spire and finished in Paris.

She always finished in Paris.

Wracked with a sob, Ava bent over herself when she finished the piece, tears in her eyes as she waved to the crowd, all on their feet.

Faye showed Callum.

"Now you know," she whispered, barely catching him thank her before she shut off the phone.

———

"Mister Gray?"

Callum held the phone against his ear with his shoulder. "Call me Callum, Mister Brooks. So great to finally talk to you."

Behind him, Brynn barreled through the door and dropped a newspaper onto the stack of mail in Callum's hands.

He gave his old friend the finger.

"Callum, I wanted to reach out to you personally. Your pieces speak to me on a level that other budding young artists have yet to reach. You paint with such story, with such lore. You're an asset to the art world. It was an honor to even receive your pieces for submission."

Callum raised a finger to his lips at Brynn, heartbeat racing. "That's a really big compliment, Mister Brooks. Thank you."

"All that is to say that I am extremely happy to invite you to our artists' residency program in Brooklyn. We'd love to highlight your work in an exhibit entitled 'Ava,' revolving around the title piece."

"Are you kidding? Sir, I—"

Sorting through the mail in his hands, Callum broke off when he came across a package. Inside were a leather journal and a thick ivory envelope, postmarked from familiar names and a foreign address.

Lucas O'Reilly and Ava Rios. You are cordially invited to join— "Mister Gray?"

Ava Rios in celebrating her matrimony to— "Are you still there?"

Callum slid the invitation over to Brynn, who mouthed expletive after expletive upon further inspection.

"I'm here," Callum finally said. "Sorry about that. "I, um, I'm very interested. But I'd like to take some time to think about the logistics of it all. Maybe we can set up a meeting?"

Callum stared down at the cardstock and ribbon.

At this point, he didn't know if fate preferred them together or apart.

"I'll be in town for a wedding."

trois

Ava always thought she might get married in a scarlet red gown or another burning color, uncanny in the middle of a forest, wicker chairs and brave new love in a place that the maps forgot.

She counted bobby pins in the musty backroom of a pretty church, bells clanging something empty as she pricked herself with one.

"And then she fell into a million-year slumber," Ava murmured.

"Hey Cinderella."

She startled, then smiled, gaze catching on Faye's reflection.

"Hey you."

Faye draped her arms over Ava's shoulders, pressing their cheeks together in the mirror.

"I haven't seen anything so wonderful since I met some awful little girl who stole the last cherry pop in the second grade, then tried to convince me that the cherry pop was made out of frozen blood anyway and that she should have it, since she was part of an elaborate coven of vampires."

Ava tossed her head back, the shaking in her hands halting for a millisecond before picking back up again.

"God, I really liked cherry," she said, "Sue me." They both laughed something older and foreign, the ghosts of the girls they'd once been dissipating with every beat.

Faye squeezed her shoulder. "You're getting married, loser." A pause. "Scared?"

Ava glanced away, dropped her voice to a dramatic hush. "Terrified."

She was only half-kidding. But Faye didn't follow up with her usual eye-roll or parental lecture. She just smiled nervously, toyed with her own plain purple gown, darker than the rest for the Maid of Honor.

Ava frowned. "What's up?"

Faye hesitated for a second before whispering, "Promise you won't hate me?"

"Why would I—"

"Ava."

The voice cut into her—down to the bone. The reaction Callum's presence brought out in Ava was always embarrassingly obvious. Her shoulders rose, her body perked like a serpent to song. Her heartbeat thrummed an old tune, blood clawing its way towards her flushed skin.

He stood there in a navy-blue suit, black ink spiraling down his arms out from underneath his white dress shirt, rolled at the sleeves. No tie, black leather sneakers on, hair combed back the color of warm honey, dressed like he might have been if this were the wedding it was supposed to be.

His knuckles were still poised over the doorframe as if he'd been about to knock but thought better of it.

Faye put her hands on Ava's shoulders, momentarily blocking Callum from her sight.

"Okay, listen. If you need to be mad at me for the rest of our lives, I understand. But Ava…you know how doubtful I was of him, of this. You've always known that. But the way you two have clung onto each other over the years defies everything that's ever made sense to me about love." Faye exhaled, hanging her head. "And I couldn't live with myself as your best friend if I hadn't made sure that you were sure."

Ava inhaled, glanced up at the ceiling, then back at Faye.

Faye paled. "Shit. I did the wrong thing." Blinking back a tear, Ava shook her head, gripped Faye's arm.

They pressed their foreheads together, and she whispered, "Thank you." And then, "Give us a minute."

Faye nodded. In her peripheral vision, Ava saw her give Callum a passing smile on the way out the door before it shut.

The silence threatened to swallow them whole.

Callum was looking at everything but her—gaze raking over the fresh lilacs and pristine table runners, the makeup spilled behind her on the vanity, the toe of one ivory shoe.

But when he finally did look at her, she understood why he hadn't. His features twisted with an emotion she'd never seen on him before—something melancholy and beautiful and tragic, like the window of a train with a beautiful view. Like a one-way ticket. Like knowing you could never go back home.

Callum rewove every thread and bead of her dress with his eyes, finally settling on her face. He cleared his throat, took another step towards her.

"Hey you."

Ava let out a laugh devoid of any humor, just a sharp, slanted sound.

He nodded at her wedding gown. "You going out somewhere?"

This laugh sounded more like a sob. She pressed her fingers to her forehead, her face to her palms.

"Why are you here?"

He raised a brow. "I was invited."

Her heart was racing, and it was getting hot in the cramped little room. "I didn't think you would come."

Callum's chuckle sounded pained, but there was a genuine smile on his face. "That's sweet."

Ava shot him a tired look, then continued counting bobby pins.

He took a step closer. "Hey."

"Don't."

Tears shielded Ava eyes, pooled before spilling across her cheeks, created jagged slants in her beautifully crafted makeup. Callum's lips were smooth against her forehead, persistent down the slope of her cheek. She didn't look at him—not when he was kissing her chin, not when he crouched down at her front, arms folded over her knees.

Callum's fingers wrapped around Ava's, dug into the white lace covering her lap.

She shook her head. They had Paris, they had New York—she finally opened her eyes to stare down at their intertwined fingers—but they didn't have this.

"Hey," Callum repeated, one hand curling under her chin. "I want to tell you something."

Ava blinked, drew in a ragged breath. Outside, she heard Faye standing guard by the door.

"This isn't fair," Ava said.

Callum nodded and whispered, "None of this was ever fair."

He let go of her hands to slip one of his into his suit jacket, surfacing with a familiar leather-bound book and a notecard taped to the face of it. Her mouth twitched.

"A wedding present," Callum explained, his grin broken. "I didn't want to show you at first. Thought you might try to make a run for it."

Through her tears, Ava smiled. "Smart move." She took the book, finger tracing the corners of the notecard, then the spine of the very thing that had brought them together. It didn't feel so sturdy anymore.

"This is the same…" Callum nodded.

Ava exhaled another shaky breath, wiped at her cheeks. "How can I be crying over you this way, when I'm supposed to be marrying somebody else?"

Callum said nothing, just stared down at the book.

She slid her finger under the seam of the note's envelope, read what was inside.

"Because you and I were never a coincidence."

Ava frowned, held the card to her chest with one hand as the other finally flipped through the pages of the journal, only to come up blank every time. She turned and turned and turned, but not a speck of ink surfaced. She looked up at Callum, a question in her eyes.

"Riddle me this," Callum whispered, balancing himself with an arm on either side of her chair, thumbs brushing her thighs, a nervous tick. "A kid sees a beautiful girl on an airplane. And I'm talking, the most beautiful girl he's ever seen in his *life*. They have this moment, and then he's about to lose her. And he doesn't know anything other than that they're getting off this plane, she's with her mother, but he has to see her again. So he takes this ten euro journal he bought at de Gaulle that he knows she saw him with, writes his email inside the front cover, and drops it. Hopes that she's the kind of girl who would pick it up."

Ava braced herself on the chair, one hand over his. "And?"

Callum smiled. "And she was the kind of girl who picked it up." He reached up to cup her face, and she leaned into him. "Not kismet. Not coincidence. I was never chasing after this book. Day one, I was chasing after you."

"Why now?" Ava asked, pushing the book from her lap. He caught it in one hand. "Why right now? Why not before? Why couldn't this ever work then?"

"I just," Callum started, "know that neither of us have been given closure to anything in our lives. I wasn't going to be the one to leave you without letting you know what this was to me. I was wrong. I would fight for you forever. I'm going to find you in that version of the story. The one that *does* end with us."

Ava reached out to hold his face in her hands. "I *can't* say goodbye to you."

Callum straightened, pulled her hands from his face in one torturous movement. Walking backwards, he cleared his throat and ducked his head behind his arm so that she wouldn't see him cry.

He held onto the door before it swung open. "Then…I'll see you in a minute, yeah?"

It was their favorite lie.

"Yeah," she whispered to his absence. "I'll see you in a minute."

A note from Callum:

This ends on an airplane. Too many stories do.

They say that you're supposed to be with the girl who looks at you and makes you understand.

Every answer, every hidden star, every mystery etched underneath this horrible world sets alight, and you cannot return to ignorance because you'll never want to.

You're not supposed to be with the girl in whom you see yourself. You're supposed to be with the girl you see in everything else.

Ava is the whir of a jet, a screen fading to black, one-half the horizon and one-half the machine on fire flying towards it. If I'd thought the flight in was difficult, the flight home was lethal.

In the turbulence and empty seat across from mine, I kept waiting for a doctor to ask me what hurt. I kept waiting for Hades to hear me cry for Eurydice. But like we always understood, this isn't that kind of story.

Back at home, I'm sitting here, and there's no truth to excavate.

I've tasted life with her, I've endured life without her. There's nothing beyond that.

A foolish man lets her remnants haunt him. An even more foolish man holds on hope that she'll come back, doesn't keep the remains.

Which one am I?

Hold on.

There's a knock at the door.

on heartbreak

THE RECKONING

I'm writing this to you,
and the moon is begging me not to,
exhausted with collecting the bits of my broken heart
and guising them as stardust.

do you remember when we stopped at the side of
the road after driving hours into the night
to look up at the stars?

we were so small and
there were so many and
I wanted to tell you how endless this all felt then,
how infinite,
but I was afraid of handing myself over that way.

because I love you so much that my body
refuses to bend for anything else.
I love you so much that on forms
I start to write your name as my home address.

this is the most fearful thing I have ever done;
I'm covering my eyes as if I didn't pay for admission,
as if I wouldn't crawl into your woods
without a flashlight,
as if I wouldn't scale the grooves of your mountain without
even a rope to rescue me.

I picture us on the side of that same road
when we're eighty, talking about this poem,
blessing the day we continued north,
sacrificing our youth to be infinite, too.

this can't be the universe where
we end up as the almost.
I can't die as somebody you used to know.

AFTER THE BLOODBATH

you say that I'm speaking in tongues.
you call me a witch—your eyes, the stake;
the match, your judgement.

I say that you're speaking in white noise,
all that's present in an absence.

when I talk now,
it's floorboards creaking,
it's where you still walk.

(isn't love the worst haunting?)

you are what's missing
and also, what remains:
the habits,
the lingo,
the toothache.

the world doesn't end,
but ours does.

everything becomes a graveyard,
everything is a haunted house,
and I am hanging the cobwebs.

if you become something else
at the hands of someone else,
it is safe to call this murder.

it is safe to say that your body
has become a burial ground
where nothing was laid to rest.

it is safe to say that there are
dead-eyed things rattling your ribcage
and trapped inside your chest.

it is safe to say that
you are the haunter and the haunted.
every person you used to be
died in that body.
you are the stranger
in your home.

in your eyes,
the lights are flickering.
from your throat,
the howl in the attic.
every strange look on your face
someone in the dark window.

a reminder of yourself
when you think you are alone.

it is safe to say
that you are in your own possession,
a crowd of ghosts fist-fighting
for the stage of your tongue,
you are the one
waiting for yourself
at the end of the hall.

so perhaps it isn't safe
to say anything at all.

TALL TALES

the worst thing you can call me
is your Wendy.

Peter, don't tell me
that I am made of dreams
and you are made of more.

in the end, people always forget
the girl in the window.

I'm the one who loved a boy
whose heart never grew old.

I'm the one who shed my blood
to make sure this tale was told.

the story still wears your name.

MESSAGES ERASED

i. I miss you something terrible.
it feels like a bird has flown
out of my chest.

ii. one day
you will marry someone else,
and I will marry someone else;
my biggest fear is that the memory of you
will show up to the wedding
without an invitation.

iii. California is on fire,
and I picked up the phone to talk to you about it,
but we're not each other's instincts anymore.
you're not my speed dial.
you're not my anything.

iv. you were more plane
than person:
flighty
and filled with emergency exits.

v. this was always the problem:
I love in a way that kills.
you love in a way that leaves.

ERASE (5) MESSAGES?

MESSAGES ERASED.

NOTHING WAS FAIR ABOUT VERONA

let's kill ourselves first
and misunderstand each other later.

imagine a love like that:
where we could pluck up dead roses
and watch them come back to life.

we could spit up the poison,
climb down the balcony,
clean up the blood.

I would rather love you as a stranger
than mourn you as a ghost.

THE VERY LAST HIGHWAY

This is not a fairytale, just a story you've heard before. We need to remind ourselves that there's a difference.

There is a boy, and there is a girl, and they're walking up a San Francisco hill just after midnight. They're sharing a cigarette, and Girl is carrying his backpack on her back because it's easier, mumbling about how incredible it is that they were across the country just half a day ago. Boy hoists her bag up his shoulder and curses about it. They are both afraid and both pretending not to be.

Boy's credit card just got declined at the Super 8 they tried to check into.

Let's call the boy Bear.

Let's call the girl Estrella.

Ursa Major.

———

Estrella sits on the sidewalk and starts to cry.

"HOW could you have missed the email that cancelled the card you put on our reservation? That was the ONE thing I asked you to do."

Bear stares at her.

"The ONE thing, Bear."

Bear stares at her.

"It's two AM!" she shouts. A homeless man across the street laughs at her.

Still, Bear stares.

"Hello? We have no place to sleep! Two weeks across the country, and we have no car, no place to sleep, no..."

Bear laughs.

He's got a good seven inches on her, so when he laughs, his shadow quakes over her skin, masking her then letting her under the light again. She's furious. She swears that they're going to die, that they'll be killed here, right under this flickering sign, or maybe just starve to death, they haven't EATEN since yesterday because they practically had to fly themselves here on that shoddy airline, and more reasons that suddenly get swallowed by her laughter, too.

She laughs and cries against his chest, like maybe she's mourning something that isn't even dead yet.

He picks up both of their bags, and they walk three more miles into the night before they find a motel with a room open. They lay over the sheets and stare at the ceiling until morning. When they get up, they share a stale sandwich, rent a car from the San Francisco airport, and head north.

———

Estrella met Bear six months before this trip. Their first date was twenty-four hours long. They had dinner and went to see a movie. Bear was tall and nervous and just out of the military. Estrella was strange and creative but always herself. Not wanting to part, they said goodnight across the Brooklyn Bridge and in a coffee shop and on the Staten Island Ferry and up the stairs leading to the apartment she shared with the roommate she hated, then in that apartment, where they didn't sleep, just talked about nothing and watched a television show about magic tricks until the sun rose again.

Suddenly, it was the same time they'd met on the afternoon before.

It had always been Estrella's favorite story to tell, proud of the birth of them, proud of that kind of wanting.

Maybe it was a kind of begging, too.

———

"Trees-Louise!"

"Terrible."

"Tree-sus!"

"The worst!"

Bear laughs as Estrella contorts her body to lay her head on the dashboard and stare up at the aisle of redwoods.

"I've never seen trees this big in my life," she gasps, holding her camcorder out of the window whilst kicking him in the elbow with her boot. For a second, Bear swerves off the road.

"They're going to be the last thing you see, too." He tickles her ankle. "Seatbelt."

"SEATBELT," she mocks, doing as told anyway. "You have to admit, not a bad sight to be stuck in."

He agrees.

———

After the twenty-four-hour date, Bear and Estrella were a couple within weeks.

They exchanged I love you's within a month.

They were professing marriage within two.

Minutes lasted years. Missed calls from friends and family tallied up on their phones. Every weeknight and weekend, a new city, a farther road trip into the night. It was that awful, wonderful kind of love, the kind you stayed up late and missed sleep for, the kind that cared not to be stretched out and savoured. It wanted to be devoured all at once, forgetting that hunger would return again after.

If only, they pondered, there was a way to bottle up those moments, carry them around and take a sip of them anytime they wanted.

Perhaps one day, when time travel was invented, they wouldn't have to worry about it.

————

They spend more time stopping along the coast than they do driving. They end up at sweet little motels and bicker on the road and take pictures of each other with their feet dangling off cliff sides. They buy fudge from a woman who owns a shop filled with the stuff along a glass beach. For free, she tells them their fortune, and it involves a snow globe and an exit sign with no exit.

They talk about what that might mean for hours and still can't figure it out.

In the forest, there are stores that sell crystals and baubles, and there's a museum of lost things built into the trees. The backseat of their rental, which they've named BABY, gets cluttered with treasure. Gasoline pirates, they continue north and further north and play hide and seek in the mist along the beaches.

At a thrift store, they purchase evening wear for each other and have a fancy seafood dinner at a fishermen's village. Bear wears a bowtie over his T-shirt, and Estrella dons the sweatshirt they picked up at a gas station in Boonville over a nice gown.

That night, they drink whiskey on the balcony of their motel room and watch the horizon disappear into the dark. Behind them, the television reports the nightly news.

"WELL I THINK THE PROBLEM IS THAT THERE ARE PEOPLE PAYING MONEY TO WASTE EVERY TOMORROW ON YESTERDAY."

Estrella strains to hear as she catches a glimpse of a long line of people outside of what looks like a factory onscreen.

But Bear is kissing the back of her neck, and the whiskey is settling in her stomach, and that is that.

————

Bear and Estrella were not right for each other.

At least, that is what everyone told them, over and over again until it became a joke they exchanged every moment they were together.

They'd miss the showtime of the movie they wanted to go see.

IT'S BECAUSE WE'RE NOT RIGHT FOR EACH OTHER!

They packed a picnic, and it started to rain.

DAMN IT, I KNEW WE WEREN'T RIGHT FOR EACH OTHER.

As in the case of Capulets and Montagues, nothing seals the fate of doomed lovers like telling them how doomed they are.

———

When they tire of the trees, they head south again.

Passing through Berkeley, Estrella gets a nose ring, and Bear gets a tattoo.

The artist and piercer laugh about how they feel like this, meeting them, so wide-eyed and in love, is déjà vu, but maybe it's because crazy kids like them burst into their shop all the time, wanting to commemorate road trips like theirs.

"What if you hate each other in a month," the artists laugh, "you're gonna wanna stare at this all the time?"

———

Bear and Estrella were not right for each other.

Suddenly, no one had to remind them of that.

Estrella still needed an order to her chaos. Bear had a mean streak.

He ran away often, without her, and the more he pushed, the more she pulled. Their fights grew nasty and unforgiving.

They hurt each other often and learned this: You can forgive yourself for anything by doing it in the name of love.

———

All down Big Sur, they pretend they are honeymooners.

When they get to Los Angeles, maybe they even believe it. A graveyard of big dreams and plastic stars, they point and gawk at everything like children.

————

Bear lost his car to a pound. Estrella lost too much to a new life. They lost each other in the process.

One night, he mentioned California, maybe getting away for a while, and she grabbed onto the idea like a buoy at high tide.

————

Down by Palm Springs, there's so much desert that it hurts their eyes, starts showing them things that aren't really there, some sandy stage-play of tumbleweed monsters and hot sun, so they pull over at a rest stop to drink sodas and watch for rattlesnakes.

"I think we'll always live on this road," Estrella announces. "Like, you go someplace once, and because of that it's changed forever, and you're changed forever. Everything is an exchange. That moment goes on existing inside of it and inside of you."

Bear gives her a funny look.

"Like you and me," he reasons.

Estrella suddenly feels uncomfortable, looks at him as if he's another desert mirage, and gets nauseous. "I guess so."

————

A week before California, Estrella took a sip of her iced coffee and scrolled through a list of sights to see on the West Coast.

"I think this is going to be good for us," she said, mostly to herself.

Bear nodded and set his phone facedown atop a newspaper. Its headline blared: DREAM COME TRUE OR DELUSION?

"We're never gonna forget it."

————

A girl is calling Bear's phone.

One minute, Frank Sinatra is playing by the pool, the cicadas are singing backup, and Bear and Estrella are slow dancing in thrifted neon bathing suits that don't fit them quite right. One minute, stars are giggling across the sky as Bear slides his hand down Estrella's back. One minute, they're both thinking that if they can pause and stay like this forever, maybe everything will be alright.

And then a girl is calling Bear.

"It's two in the morning," Estrella announces, "on the East Coast."

Bear inhales. "It is."

"It's two in the morning, and this person is calling you."

Bear exhales. "She is."

————

I'd like to tell you that Bear and Estrella were meant to be, that they are being immortalized this way because they deserve it.

I'd like to tell you anything other than that their trip ended abruptly after that phone call. That they held on for one more awful month and fought and hissed and hurt some more because they needed to really hate each other before they could walk away. That the breakup was awful and cruel, so much that they could never speak to each other again after it.

I'd like to tell you that the cosmos, the fates, the gods, took pity and brought them back together somehow. But they didn't.

This story doesn't need any gods. There is no magic in what's true.

————

One gruelling day later, they arrive back in San Francisco. They have some hours before their flight, so they sit on the steps of Lombard Street and stare out over the city.

"I forgive you," she lies.

He kisses the side of her forehead.

"I love you," she continues. That's true.

He grabs her chin and pulls her in.

"That concludes your session for the day," he whispers against her lips.

————

Estrella gasps as the concrete and flowers harden into linoleum.

A man in a lab coat dons an unfriendly smile and pulls at something attached to her temple.

"That concludes your session for the day," he repeats, "and please do try not to make any sudden movements. You might be feeling a bit of sensory overload."

Estrella shakes.

"It can't be over. I need to go again."

"Estrella, we've gone over this," the man sighs, "more than one session per day will make you sick. Besides, I've got another appointment right after you. Quite sad, actually. A widower. Wants to relive his wedding in Tuscany. Came wearing the suit and everything, even though I told him he didn't need to dress for the part, it's all mental..."

As the man rambles on, a tear slips down Estrella's cheek. She squints at the clock on the stark white wall. It is indeed 6pm. She's spent another day, another paycheck, on the very last highway.

———

Snow Globe Studios began as a novelty experience, another stab at bringing virtual reality to the masses.

But this was no video game.

Aptly titled, one could upload their favorite memories and relive them for a pretty penny. It would be as vivid and hyper-realistic of an experience as it had been when you first lived it. It was a hit for those who'd peaked in college or lost loved ones. But especially for the heartbroken.

They flocked to the studios of their cities in crowds, at first wanting to reminisce for a short time, then going rabid like addicts, unable to savor reality when their warmest memories, ones that they could count on, could be relived over and over again.

It was Estrella's fifth visit that month.

———

The next day, Estrella's hand twitches against her side.

She taps her foot impatiently. In her purse, her phone is ringing.

She ends the call without answering it. The bank leaves her another message about that personal loan.

When her name is called, she shoots out of her seat.

Inside, the same man who unplugged her the day before, plugs her in again. He asks her to count backwards from ten. Slowly, the fluorescent lights become stars.

Bear takes back his credit card.

Estrella sits on the sidewalk and starts to cry.

THE WEEKEND FORECAST

I hate that I still check your horoscope
whenever I check mine.

I want to be your chance encounter
with an old ghost.

I want to be the door reopened;
I want to be the revisit,
rebirth,
regrowth you need when Venus passes through.

I still check your horoscope
whenever I check mine,
and I hate it,
begging the stars to make room for me
in your fate.

GIVING TREE

what have I become
at your hands?
or rather,
what have I
unbecome?

the apple was ripe,
the branches, some sturdy,
but you ask me
what are you supposed to do
now that you're down to the stump?

the women in my life
are all giving trees,
cautionary tales.

the women in my life are jack-in-the-boxes,
wind us up until we pop,
run in fear of where you pushed us.

I don't know,
we joked that we were both flighty,
both a little bit wild
both bracing for impact,
but you were plane
and I was tarmac—

I know you don't understand poetry,
so this means:
I will wear you forever,
and you are already heading
for another place to land.

MONTHS

December crisping into January,
and I slipped on the ice of your heart. eyes the dead of winter,
words the warm call of a wood fire, and I'm burning cold, cold,
cold.

February's paper cut hearts and one-time darlings. the bouquet
in me was dead in the vase of your calloused hands. in the
end, love bites are just bruises.

March and April,
I blossomed under your beckoning, ripened in a garden of
bedsheets. you were a gardener, and my body was a bent rose
stem; I guess your green thumb sprouted something in me.

May June July
was a blur of sweat and concrete, you called me your
firecracker but only let me shine on the fourth. three months
too fast; they say you feel the most alive right before you die.

flaming August,
just us and the dog days. you wrapped me in a chokehold and
laughed about it, bits of the sun stuck in your teeth. I sweltered
and smiled; now there are burn marks on my heart.

September October,
come here and change our colors; we fought like hot crimson
and bled over the green we grew. after Halloween, you were
still a ghost.

November,
the cold crept up and you tied me down in lace and wet ribbon,
cranberry lips and a ripped coat, you left me wanting and
waiting on a street corner alone. I cried and the world sang,
it's the most wonderful time of the year.

December crisping into January,
sometimes euphoria is just a fever;
the year begins with broken bottles and not you.

THE ELEPHANT IN THE ROOM /
AN ELEPHANT NEVER FORGETS

this poem is a funeral.

I am filling a casket with metaphors and keepsakes;
here lies all I thought we'd be.
we gather here today to mourn
everything that was once the best thing.

I can no longer rob my own grave;
I cannot relive the fire by kneeling at its embers.

I don't need a reminder;
I need to be brave enough to remember.

DEAR ORPHEUS

dear Orpheus,
if hell is my heaven
and heaven is called home,
would you still burn yourself alive
to keep me warm?

dear Orpheus,
it's okay here,
for Hades sings me awake at night;
my demons know me better
than anyone else.
I can see the dead,
and they all have your eyes.

dear Orpheus,
I once told you,
"I am going to die here" and
you were ready to say, "no, you won't"
when you realized that I was pointing
to the center of your chest.

dear Orpheus,
don't worry, every ring of hell
is a fine piece of real estate.
I vacation in limbo
and summer in lust.

dear Orpheus,
I have sent you burnt postcards
and yet you still cry.
"wish you were here;
I finally feel alive."

BREAKING UP WITH EURYDICE

no more, my love,
enough.

the sun is setting on my strength,
and my bones are breaking
from the weight
of caging two hearts in.

I would die for you,
but I cannot live like this.
I have been staring too hard into the abyss,
just so that the truth won't hurt your eyes.

and it has left me blind,
it has left me blind.

I know we once swore
that our demons would die soon;
I know we once swore to
see this through.

but I can go no further than the dark,
and I have spilled too much blood
to make you feel full.

I suppose,
when you asked me how far I would go,
I mistook it for a promise,
when it was a test.

I would love you ten times over,
but I will never love you this way again.

RABBIT HOLES

I'm sorry for the things I said when
the moon was full.

it's funny,
the people and places and moments we call forever
and then never see again.

in the place where you left me,
the blood is still warm.
the faucet is still running.

there are words for this,
I know them.
I used to be filled with them.

I could not be the graveyard dirt
you used to bury
your dreams.

in the place where you left me,
the engine is still going,
the sparrows won't sing.

so strange,
falling in love with wolves,
then leaving because of the teeth.

HOW TO HEAL

one. there was a time with them that made you cry, made you avoid your own eyes in the mirror, made you think of always and expiration dates. the book they never read, the poem they laughed at, the necklace blaring the wrong birthstone.

put it in someplace obvious, someplace that'll show its teeth when it smiles. a reminder. this is the only time you're allowed to be unkind to yourself.

two. do not torture yourself with fantasies of apologies and possibilities, nor sweet serendipities. live everyday certain that it is not them at the door or on the phone or back to you at the coffee shop. live everyday sure that you will never see them again, even if it feels like one million little deaths.

because the chance of them will not heal you. find closure in the growth of your own bones.

three. it will be tempting, but do not look. I promise that you do not want to know.

four. go to the place you once thought could only be beautiful beside them. stand there and cry if you need to. but open your eyes long enough to look at how it went on, existing. that is a lesson, not a tragedy.

do not let them become the paint on the walls.

five. listen to the song you first slow danced to—firebugs, flushed cheeks, pink lips—listen to it and sing it hard and ugly. salt, wound, salt, wound. scream it off your rooftop, again and again until the lyrics are more you than you are them.

it's your song now.

six. go to the place, listen to the song, do not look. wash,
rinse, and repeat.

seven. one day, you will wake up and think of the mozzarella
sticks you'll have for lunch or the reality television show you
fell asleep watching last night, and then it'll make you sob,
that random thought you had.

because, for the first time in forever, it wasn't them.

eight. clear the nightstand, remove the bandage. you do not
need to be unkind. you do not need the reminder.

on self

PROCLAMATION

I will not stop.
I will call down the fates, I will dig up spring.
I will not tear apart this body; I will simply wake it up,
travel hundreds of miles within myself
until I've claimed every bone.

I AM

I sit down to dinner with every girl I have been,
every woman I will be.
a feast of white bread and red wine
spilling from the tables into our eager palms,
a reconciliation.

all the same brown eyes,
all in dresses like the feathers on ravens,
like the color of bone.

at the children's table,
five asks eight if Mom and Dad are going to make it.
sixteen and I weep.
seventeen's bones prod her skin
when she says she's not hungry,
and thirty holds her like a mother would a child, belly full.

ten twines my hair in braids, then scowls
when twenty-five unravels them.
on me, thirteen's birthmarks have become bruises,
red scars lightening white,
handprints the color of ghosts.

around the table, aging up,
we whisper the names of people
who have promised us forever.
around the table, aging down, we whisper,
gone, gone, gone.

I fold myself into tight embraces,
eighty yelling that it is beautiful where she is,
and my hands ache for her like a mountain climb.
twelve asks if we're going to be okay;
I tell the truth or lie when I say

that we're just fine.

there are nights I mourn them more
than I can celebrate myself.
there are nights they seem farther away
from me than I can reach,
clinging onto snakeskin
like a winter coat.

but too long are the lengths
I have gone to earn these bones to give up now.
for I am a wildfire;
my sole purpose is to grow.

CASUALTIES

some people are born at war with themselves—
this, the duel on the hill of becoming.

you come into this world with a battle cry
and grow into your declaration,
grow into your fight.

frontlines of skin and fortresses of bone;
you stab yourself each time
you beg to be someone else.

you imagine them as feral dancers and their two routines
to the same song,
Could Be and *Must Be*,
Because Of and *In Spite Of*,
heroine and villain,
poison and elixir,
shadow and light.

every time you love a love that leaves,
you recruit another soldier into an army
that fights inside of you but will not fight for you.
you are riddled with exit wounds;
still inviting, "come enlist!"

it's okay, you'll take a shot of whiskey, and you'll feel better,
and in the morning when you feel worse you'll take a shot,
and you'll feel better—
everything that helps you must also hurt you
or it doesn't work.

one would think: you know the plan,
you must also know the defense.

one would think: you know the path to safety,
you must also know detours.

this will not make textbooks, only diaries, only memory.
what satisfies the victor
when the defeated stands in the mirror?
on this quest, the bloodshed runs within you and
only your losses will let you win.

in the morning you check for casualties—
the relief and the sadness:
all the dead bodies laid out
are you.

YOU DON'T FEEL VERY SPECIAL

you don't feel very special, but this world
went pliant just to give you room to be.
the many different people you will become
already live inside of you
like nesting dolls taking turns in the light.
you write a story, and its ending can
be found deep inside of the beginning—
prophecies never know to call themselves prophecies,
like Benvolio telling Romeo of rank poison.
there is no miracle in a seed that sprouts,
it is born knowing what it is supposed to do;
you are born knowing what you are supposed to do—
do not step outside of your body, looking for answers,
be done begging to become someone new,
surrender yourself,
dig into your soul like wet clay, for molding.

SKIN

I have been the girl in the red dress,
red dress on the floor
next to her pride, makeup running.

I have been the pedestal and
the marble on it.

I have been the glass half full,
half empty,
half broken,
thrown at the wall.

I have been the bullet,
I have been the wound,
I have been everything that it took
to become neither.

I have always wanted the road;
I have been a tire-marked soul.

I have picked the roses
that stem from my chest,
given them away,
then blamed them for dying.

I have been the sinner,
the saint,
no religion,
every religion,
godless, god herself.

I have been so much of him,
of her,
that I became the mask of me.

I have been the bluebird,
I have been blue.

I have been scars, ink, birthmarks,
broken bones, bruises,
smoke, hair dye, and lipstick.

change the paint on the walls;
I am still home.

AFTER INSIDE OUT

in a locked room with my emotions,
I am sitting pale and open,
and they are pulsing,
vibrant,
wanting things,
all different people who look exactly like me.

pale pink *contentment* insists that she is different
from her neighbor *happiness*,
who is all neon and gap-toothed.

contentment runs her fingers
through my hair but will not let it loose.

"I am for Sunday mornings," she tells me,
then points at happiness,
"she is for the rest of your life."

NESTING BEASTS

I am finally the girl
I wrote about becoming
in my diary when I was thirteen years old.

the views are great here,
I just didn't expect it to be so cold.

I am always cutting myself open,
delivering myself to the next dream.

I am a matryoshka doll,
always nesting.

always waiting for the day
there isn't anymore
to pull out from inside of me.

GARDEN STATE

if the mind is a garden,
then mine is overgrown—
desperate and uncertain
of how it belongs to this world.

crows and sparrows
lured to the birdhouse with crumbs
have learned to get through the netting.
they stole away my crops
and for some eras of my life,
I was always starving,
always mending, always forgetting.

if the mind is a garden,
I let the wildflowers reign—
to grow without pattern,
ignorant of consequence and simply born;
my thoughts the roses—
pretty and having
forgotten their thorns.

if the mind is a garden,
I've spent too much time lost in it.
things are familiar,
but I still don't know my way around—
there is sting and there is honey,
and without knowing any better,
both long to be found.

if the mind is a garden,
I must apologize for its quiescence,
for its raised beds,
all the times I rebelled against my own growth,
all the times I surrendered my own head.

if the mind is a garden,
then I suppose
I should tend to its lushness,
I should plant more bulbs,
and set down the mulch,
and lay in it barefoot.

I should wander far and find
the world's trowels,
underplant my quiet thoughts
deep beneath affirmations
with sturdy barks.

I should perhaps forget Eden,
let it breathe,
let it tangle,
let it flower,
let it sin.

I should keep it open
but keep aware
of who I let in.

A LOVE LETTER TO THOSE WHO LOOKED MY EATING DISORDER IN THE EYE BEFORE I COULD

did you say malnourished?
I think I heard milestone.

the worry in your voice
sounded as sharp as applause;
another victory dinner that
I couldn't eat.

of course, we became friends.
like me, anorexia was always hungry.
like me, she had teeth.

I was a blind woman
reading the braille of my spine,
my rib cage,
my collar bones,
like some kind of truth.

but I want you to know that I got better,
took down the funhouse mirror,
took up more space in the room.

I want you to know that my mind
is a safe place to live now,
that my hair isn't the only thing that has body,
that these bones which once were a prison
are now called home.

that I have never been prouder
to be bad at math;
no altar at the scale,
no caloric algebra to count out on skeleton bones.

I want you to know that I am no longer
the coldest thing in the room.

I am both the gardener
and the rose.

I am in bloom.

AUDITION

I am here to audition for my namesake:
the role of Naiche (noun: *mischief-maker*)

Puerto Rican,
Native American,
Black girl.

I am here to audition as myself.

but I will not perform for you.
no monologue,
no costume,
no dressing room of accents.

just my existence,
just my hands,
just the land
and how it trusts me,
just my potluck diction,
just the way I read my books
and the way I curl my tongue,
just my skin as it holds me,
just my dreams,
and all of my grandparents' stories.

I have spent too long trying out for a role
that has always been mine,
always fed a line
then turned away, not enough *this* or *that*
inside a life of which I am its star.

just another way to keep a hand around a throat:
deciding who a person must be
in order to prove who they are.

CATCHING UP

I love you,
but unbind me.

your first always
becomes folklore;
I have stuffed my cheeks with breadcrumbs,
desperate to leave you behind me.

I love you,
but untie me.

I'm no good at necromancy;
we can't keep resurrecting this dead union
and pretending that it's fate.

my darling,
please release me.
let people see that I am more
than just the consequence of you.

I want to be a legend,
not a lesson,

the girl who knew how to leave,
good at goodbyes,
the girl who grew.

TEN SECRETS

I feel at home in horror; I do not mind the teeth.

As a child playing games, I was always curious, always
wondering, always chased. I was quiet but never patient
enough to hide.

In our high school senior yearbook, I was voted most likely
to be a runaway bride.

A map of New York City is just my second body.

I can tell you where the scars are, where I became most
beautiful, which streets I wish didn't know my name.

My mind never accepts that the door is closed, I have to
check the knob three times.

What I'm saying is, I'd still run away with him if he asked.
but he's never asked.

There are still cracks in the crescent moon mirror from that
one delirious winter; my reflection is changed forever.
It was two months too long to call it a bender.

And I still keep the cigarettes in the left drawer, and the
ruined dress at the back of the closet, and all my bad habits
are in the waste bin of my chest, but I never empty the trash.

I think fresh air tastes better when it's a relief from drowning.

Somewhere along the stretch of Big Sur there is a video
camera I lost on a rock, on a cliff, on some other me's version
of forever.

Which means I am immortalized this way.

Which means I hate a stranger who has the good bits of the movie and will never know how it ends.

There was a time my father was staring at me for so long that I thought he was admiring me. I was young, so I didn't know the difference between admiration and inspection.

"You're pretty enough to be an actress, but first you'd have to get those teeth fixed."

These were the only compliments my father knew how to give me, criticism gift-wrapped with a compliment. The only green thumb my father ever had, reaching in to sprout something awful in me.

Up until then, I never thought about my open mouth. Before that day, I used to smile like sunshine, like I was about to take a bite out of the world. For the next five years, I wouldn't know how my teeth looked in a photo or on a first date, his words falling over me like thread.

That thread sewing my lips shut.

Sometimes I want a life outside of this life. A small town where I can put my pen down. I don't love instantly and incessantly.

A hello is a hello, a goodbye is a goodbye, and then I make dinner and go to bed.

None of it becomes poetry.

NOTHING RHYMES WITH ORANGE

he told me that I was like
the word orange because I made no sense,
never did allow myself to be cloaked by one label—
fruit or color,
girl or monster.

I ripened under the sun, and he peeled bits and pieces
of my skin away until he could admire my jagged insides,
bittersweet nectar that was neither feeble nor intoxicating.

he told me that I was like the word orange
because I was picked and used so often,
consumed and enjoyed, bitten and destroyed.

but I never did rhyme with any other string of letters.

I never did find harmony with anyone else.

THINGS THAT ARE WRONG WITH ME

I am the queen of hearts,
a heart of debts
with those who only
ever come collecting.

I'll let you live in me
(rent-free!),
always the one with beds to spare,
room to give,
extra to eat.

I am a magician at making myself
disappear in your presence,
dealing out second chances like playing cards
even though I already know
which one you'll choose.

I want to be kept so badly
that I'd hand my soul over to anyone
with room in the backseat.

I want to be loved so badly
that I'd drink the poison just to die full.

BECOMING

my hands are full
with all the poetry I cannot write.

I am molten;
I am decaying.

I weep at the grave
of the girl I was before the pen.

there is nothing romantic
about my mind.
I dress my words in pink
and shout the names of my lovers
until they rhyme.

I am paper,
I am endless,
what a curse,
to never die.

but everyone wants to love a writer.

like blood and ink,
they always want you until you stain.

DUAL

I ran after myself,
but I could not keep up.
I ran from myself,
but she's the one who knows me best.
I ran into myself,
I keep running into myself.

this is a lifetime of setting out clothes
for whichever girl I will wake up as in the morning.

the only way I can describe it:
one minute the beast is chasing me.
the next minute,
I am the beast.

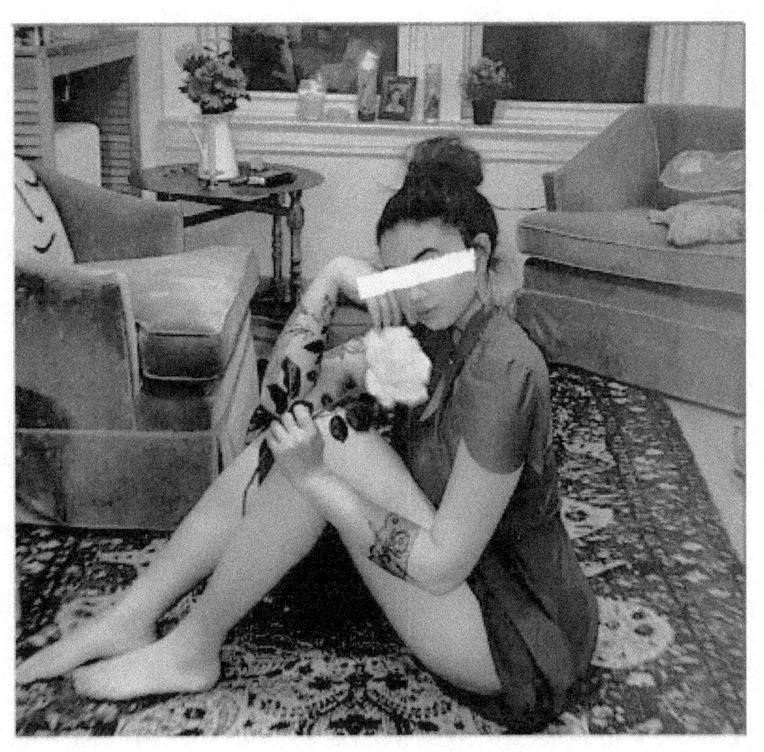

on magic

TOIL AND TROUBLE

things that are spells:
a turned page,
my mother's phone number,
the breath between our first kiss
and second kiss.

your name,
my own name,
the name of the first thing I ever wanted
so badly I could die
and how I shouted it from everything
but my tongue.

waking up (a new morning),
an open door (a slamming one),
the words "love, hate, and wait"
always in that order.

a trembling of the bottom lip,
the people who are chariots, and
the first thing I ever said to you.

how it changed everything,
how it decided my fate,
how I barely remember it.

TAROT CARD GOTHIC

eight of cups—you are full but you are fragile. you rise but
you are waning. upright, a celestial plane bows to you.
reverse, God has her tongue down your throat.

queen of swords—see how this blade is being climbed by
roses. see how this blade turns blood to pomegranate juice.
see how this blade brings death and nothing else. every time,
there is still a blade.

the lovers—the heart is a mirror. we look into it to see
ourselves. perhaps those who don't know themselves will
never recognize what they're in love with.

knave of pentacles—a blackbird travels back to the nest to
secure its future. a row of sirens wait in line to drown before
they can breathe. only today can explain tomorrow.

three of wands—something that is waiting. something that is
holding its breath. some god that is not our god playing chess
with his country. you miss the corners of the map the closer
you are to it.

the star—you are soaked in your own light. you are growing
because of and in spite of yourself. yes, that taste in your
mouth is magic. the night turns to silk just to dress you. you
feel as though you are being chased.

the moon—you are chasing the star.

WITCH BOY

witch boy,
broomstick baby,
sliver-moon smile,
candlewick bravado,
greedy with your magic,
walking superstition.

I'll call down the lightning,
make ghosts of the living,
turn flesh into altar,
speak to you in spells.

son of midnight—
come lay down your enchantment,
summon the storm
and the stags
and whatever else hides within me.

the fiend I've put my faith in,
the curse that I'll allow.

HOW TO LOVE A PIRATE

1. pledge allegiance to the Jolly Roger. your spine is
    now a mast.
2. become a treasure that will not be stolen.
3. become a stranger to the shore.
4. collect your tears in bottles and present the bottles as
    gifts. it will remind them that you contain the sea.
5. learn to swallow rum like water.
6. no matter how often they beg you, do not find a home
    at the tip of their sword. do not parrot their fury.
7. protect your heart from looting.
8. do not walk the plank.

BATTLE STRUNG

The potholes were playing Stairway to Heaven.

Rave eyed them for a moment, the flame on her cigarette jetting to the finish. It burned her, and she cursed, prying her gaze away from the guitar riffs screaming out from under the city, the hands and silver eyes slipping out from beneath the darkness.

All on a street with no name, in an alleyway with no story. At least, not to this world.

There was a fresh burn mark the shape of a bullet hole in her favorite leather jacket now, the one patched up with memoirs of concerts past, slashed twice at the back like coin slots.

"Hell," she rasped.

Rave stubbed the thing out with the heel of one boot, crawling over the concrete to lift the metal slab before slipping right in.

Rather than sinking into fresh sewage or pitch blackness, she rose on the same street.

Or, a reflection of it.

all along the watchtower

It was the Lower East Side, but not.

Barely a soul on the sidewalks, sky gray and spitting lightning without rain, cars revving go on red, and a rickety bar venue's neon sign flickering off and on like a beacon. It hummed. *Dog. of. The. Hair.*

Inside, it always reeked of the night before. Disgusting to the average human, perhaps. But when she was above ground, wings bound tightly to her back and aching to be strum as she couriered dry cleaning around the city on her bike, Rave wished she had it bottled as a perfume. She found a stool, slung her jacket on the one beside her, and let her braids unravel from atop her head.

She stretched her arms out, and her wings mirrored the action. They were made of maple wood, as her mother's had been, rich brown cut across by stark white strings—the veins. When she shifted the slightest bit, a small tune would escape and land upon her brown shoulders like a songbird.

Up above, budding human musicians were saving up pennies for a guitar, and she had two sprouting from her shoulder blades. One wing knocked over a bottle of hot sauce when she went to snap for the barkeep, Joe. An angry riff sounded from it.

Burly old Joe, seeming to have woken from his slumber, hobbled out and wiped a speck of grease from his neck with a kerchief. His smile was missing one tooth.

"Hey, Yoko."

Rave drummed her fingers on the counter. "Don't call me that."

Joe chuckled and poured her a rum and coke. "If the wings fit, honey."

He knocked on the wood behind the bar, where it used to read, *Home of the Scarlet Three,* her own brooding face plastered between those of two startlingly gorgeous twin boys, Dice and Ensley Rough. Now, they were split in two: Ensley announcing the Crooks and Thieves on tonight. Dice inviting the masses for a Leather Bullets show on Thursday. She was nowhere to be seen.

Except perhaps in the music that was flooding into the bar from the basement, leaking out from the side door and pooling at her feet. *I don't want to love you from a chokehold, I don't want to start another fight. I can't light a fire just to make you see the light.*

Her lyrics. A man's voice.

So, if you want to go, then goodnight.

Rave pursed her lips to brace herself before downing the rest of her drink.

"Nice chat," she called to Joe, whose eyelids were once again forgetting their stance. She ducked towards the door and opened it, letting her song burst into the room.

"You're playing a dangerous game, double agent."

Rave paused at the top step. "You don't know what game I'm playing."

Joe drowsily played a little tune on his own banjo back and exhaled a wisp of smoke. "Hey kid, don't let those boys turn you into something you don't know how to be."

"It's a little late for that."

smells like teen spirit

Down the steps, she held the walls for balance and squeezed her wings into the narrow passage, thrust into an underbelly of grit and bones, slanted and dirtied photo frames lining the pathway. In one photo, Steven Tyler was playing his keyboard wings on Dog of the Hair's stage.

The bottom of the steps led to one final hallway. At the end of it, a bulb shook with the bass. A sign on a lonely door read: IN SESSION. DO NOT ENTER.

Another one: RADIOACTIVE BABES MAY BE OF HARM.

Rave turned the knob so hard it nearly broke off.

Ensley sat on an ivory couch, nearly bodiless with his white coat blending in. Lightning bolts, jet black as his mane, were embroidered on the shoulders of it. His wings, angel white, were the source of the song, but she could barely see them behind his two guests.

On either side of him were two humans, faux angel wings from a party supply store strapped pathetically to their leaning shoulders.

One T-shirt read *Crook*, the other read *Thief*, with a heart scrawled on the side of it. Ensley clearly hadn't gotten the memo, for he was bare-chested.

Rave unplugged his amp, hooked like an IV to one wing.

Ensley glanced up and beamed when he saw her, bright and pure to the ignorant.

Rave cocked her head at the girls. "Ladies. Goodbye."

Befuddled, they glanced at Ensley for permission. Still smiling at Rave, he flicked his hands at the exit. They'd barely slipped through before she shut the door behind them.

"My darling," Ensley cooed, scooting over on the couch. His chest glittered from somebody's iridescent eyeshadow. Perhaps his own. "Come and sit."

"I'm not staying long. I just can't help but feel intrigued when I hear somebody covering one of my songs."

Ensley smiled again, leaning forward on the sofa. He reached for her hand and pressed it against his cheek, her stack of rings indenting the skin just above the line of his jaw.

"Darling, I was short for my setlist."

Rave laughed, but there was no smile in it. "So, you stole my song."

"Borrowed..."

"Hm, is that the name of your album? You've done quite a bit of that."

"Love, you leave genius sitting on your nightstand, and someone's going to snatch it up."

It comes back to her in flashes: fireball whiskey, her wings bristling against naked, hot, shivering skin, humming the notes of Dreams with every stroke.

The painful morning light. Her songbook open on the nightstand. The sweet parting kiss she'd mistaken for more than a honey trap.

"Well who am I to keep you down?"

Rave shut her eyes and breathed out through her nose.

"Perhaps I can make it up to you," Ensley continued, standing to stagger them both against the wall. Her eyes kept closed as he whispered her own lyrics against her neck, kissing there, a slit of the throat. But the kiss drew no blood. It was soft, and she allowed it, as one does when the chessboard is still full.

Rave held her breath. Her lyrics, his kiss, the cold wall. She tried to think of honey and lilac and something good.

livin' on a prayer

Rave is a young girl.

It's five years prior, and the two most beautiful boys Under York are looking for a bandmate. She's lined up behind twenty other girls donning ripped jeans and heavy eyeliner and a penchant for rock and roll.

"She's it," Ensley announces. He says it so softly, so unspectacularly, Rave is stunned. She's barely finished her first verse when the decision is made. The rest of the girls are sent home.

She feels prophetic, like a chosen one. Her boots knock against one another. She has butterflies.

Dice nods slowly. In two months, they will be renowned underground. Tongues will burn with their names on them. *The Scarlet Three.*

When the twins take either one of her hands, she savors this moment, the one she will remember as her invention, her birth.

How little we remember of the disciples before their last supper.

"What else do you have for us, love?"

How we mistake lights in the night for angels, when they are factories.

thunderstruck

Back above ground on Astor Place, Dice welcomed her into her own apartment.

Exhausted, she narrowed her eyes and brushed past him. "Hadn't a clue that we hired a doorman."

Her roommate, Amira, poked her head out from their kitchen. Her curls were frazzled, and the oversized frames she wore clung to the bridge of her nose for dear life. Freckles constellated around them. For a moment, the easy swagger in Rave's step faltered. Her wings bristled against their bindings.

"Apparently," Amira called, "but I'm not tipping him."

Rave smiled.

"I don't think you can give me the kind of tip I'm looking for," Dice called out. Rave tensed. His breath was hot against the back of Rave's neck. He lowered his voice to a hush. His black fingernails dug into the side of her arm. "But I think you do, Rae."

"You're missing a V."

Dice laughed, brashly and broken, so different from his brother's light jest. They were snow and rain, delicate and sharp, opposite sides of the same coin. But both downpours in their own right.

The spikes atop his head looked like weapons in this light.

"C'mon, let's go to your room."

Rave clenched her fist. "I'll pass."

"You're kidding."

"You're right. I'm all out of songs, so I'm pursuing stand-up."

Dice frowned. The crow tattooed by his eye wrinkled into a shapeless smear. "You know I'm not—"

"Leave."

"So *he* can just—"

"Leave now." Her wings were desperate now, thrashing. Clashing chords escaped from beneath her jacket. "Song factory's closed. Indefinitely."

Dice's eyes flashed red for a moment, but Rave stood her ground until he softened, pasted on that leering smile, and jostled her shoulder.

"Y'know it's just jokes." He kissed her on the cheek. She turned to stone. "How 'bout I leave for now? Come back later?"

"Sure," Rave replied. "Yeah. Whatever. As long as you get on the leaving part."

Dice snorted. "I like it when you bite."

When she closed the door behind Dice, Rave pressed her forehead against it, the tension in her body finally unraveling. When she turned, Amira was standing before her, proffering a slice of pizza. The look on her face didn't match the sweet gesture.

Rave bit into the slice without touching it. Her lips brushed the tips of Amira's fingers for a moment. She swallowed. Amira was still scowling.

"What?"

"Ensley was over last night."

"Mhm."

"Nearly passed by Dice on his way out..."

"Okay."

Amira sighed as Rave spoke with her mouth full, finishing the slice in one final giant bite.

"What are you doing with those losers, Rave?"

Rave threw her jacket on the ground and slumped onto their sofa. Amira joined her and delicately placed Rave's feet in her lap.

"Unfortunately, not much."

Rave watched Amira's curls jostle each other this way and that as she shook her head.

"I wish you would stand up for yourself and just—"

"I wish *you* would stop playing my keeper."

"I'm not your keeper, I'm your roommate. Which means that I care—"

"Well, don't."

"You know, you could live like a queen underground. You *choose* to live in this shitty apartment with me." Amira sat up, scooting Rave's feet until they thumped against the floor. Rave groaned, letting one wing out, and lifted up beside her.

Feeling mean, Rave muttered under her breath, "Sometimes I wonder why." Feeling very mean, she continued, "What are you, *jealous*?"

The silence was deafening. Rave was Brutus, but she was also the one bleeding out.

But ever soft, Amira simply pushed the glasses up her nose and returned Rave's venom with a smile.

She said, "God, you're like a razor blade. You know that?"

Rave relaxed, grateful that Amira was more than what she deserved. She raised a brow. "Were you the kind of kid who played with sharp objects?"

Amira pulled Rave in for a hug, and Rave inhaled the sweetness.

"Honey and lilac," Amira explained, "shampoo."

Rave nodded.

And something good.

sweet emotion

The night of Dog of the Hair's big showcase, Rave dreamt of girls. Girls with buzzcuts, girls with bloody lips, girls like petals—soft and falling. Girls in dense crowds with strange and pretty faces, girls wearing short skirts, leather clinging onto them for dear life, and girls in white nightgowns like ghosts or just conservatives. They were all around her, circling her bed in some sort of ritual—thin lips, wide eyes, bleached hair, dark skin, oval faces, strong jaws, fruity perfume, whiskey breath—staring over sleeping form. Protecting. Threatening, maybe.

One girl broke through the hive to reach down and cup her chin. She was singing her a song. One that Rave had written. She'd only ever heard it on a man's tongue. So really, she'd never heard it sung.

The girl leaned over, and her curls came to life. They caressed Rave.

They became a noose around her throat.

Rave woke up suddenly, breathing heavy, and swore in her dark reflection that she saw all of the girls become very small and disappear into the caverns of her gaping mouth. She glanced over at the clock, and it screamed at her in blaring red.

In an hour, she and Amira were dressed in gold and dark denim on the downtown D train. A few men leered at them from across the car. Rave adjusted one of the spikes at her hipbone, the shredded Harley tee riding up her midriff. A mother made a nasty face and pulled her son into her chest, ironically using her own bosom as a shield.

Rave and Amira leaned into each other and laughed.

They arrived at the pothole just before dusk, and only a drunk Wall Street wolf took a second glance as the two gorgeous girls disappeared into the sidewalk. Rave held onto Amira's bare hip as the world turned upside down. It had to be this way, a fae's touch like the swipe of a MetroCard. Rave was used to this method of transport, already her wings were rustling in their bindings, playing excited and clashing notes like puppies at the jingle of a leash, but the magic instantly bore down on her roommate without mercy.

"Just a little nauseous," Amira murmured. She was jostled by a person clad solely in neon green, electric wings covering Bowie as they strutted into Dog of the Hair. A line was already forming outside. Amira apologized and stumbled backwards. "Maybe a little nervous."

Rave frowned. "Why? You've done this a dozen times."

"And every time, I've gotten that look—" Amira stared pointedly at two women donning jet black wings and chain-smoking cigarettes in front of the bar. They were staring at Amira and her smooth shoulder blades with blatant disgust.

Rave stepped in front of her and gave the pair a middle finger each.

"I don't belong here, Rave. Ever since you let me into your world, I've felt like Wendy in Peter Pan, or something. Sometimes I still can't accept that all of this is real." Amira blushed and some of the glitter shook out of her hair. "And you know that I love being your groupie..."

"You're *not*—"

Amira raised a hand to stop her. "By *choice*."

Rave glanced down at her black utility boots, scuffing the heels, and smiled.

"I just worry—"

"Doll!"

Rave startled as a heavy arm landed across her shoulders, painfully pinning down her braids. She winced. Ensley smelled like suntan lotion and heavy cologne but dressed like starlight, flashes of silver darting across his jet-black suit. When they were young, the band was still together, and she still saw signs of life behind his pretty eyes, she might have called him her dark angel, and he'd have laughed. He'd have kissed her on the cheek, and they'd have written a song about it. Dice would have loved it. They'd get drunk and play it over and over again until their three voices sounded like one.

Rave shrugged away.

"What is it? I've got to go in, do soundcheck."

"That's just it, love. I've got news for you," Ensley smiled that used car salesman smile, and something rotted in the pit of her stomach. He glanced over her shoulder, to where Amira was scratching at her arm and adjusting her disco slip. The smile froze on his face. "You bring your pet? Can't leave her off a leash 'round these parts." Ensley laughed. "She might get impounded."

A second passed, and Rave had him by the collar, shoving him backwards into the street.

"You don't talk to her like that."

Ensley grimaced, straightening his suit. "I was *only* kidding. You know that." He nodded at Amira. "She knows that, yeah?"

Amira squinted her eyes at him.

"You have five seconds," Rave sighed, "and then you've lost my interest."

Ensley smirked. "You're in."

Rave frowned. "I know I'm in. I'm on in thirty."

"No, you're in with *Crooks and Thieves*, pet. Your solo slot's gone to someone else. It's all been sorted. You're getting onstage with us, doing some backup vocals, getting a

231

little cheeky for the crowd. Very nostalgic, they'll love it, you'll shine. Win, win, win."

Fire coiled and snapped beneath her skin. "You didn't."

Ensley sighed and pinched the bridge of his nose like an impatient teacher dealing with a rowdy child. "Babes, I'd never let you embarrass yourself with a little indie coffee shop opening act. The early crowd and you alone? Tragic. They'll eat you alive." He placed a cold hand on her cheek, and his ring—a single angel wing—felt like it was slicing into her. "Now you're part of the main event, just like old times. Been thinking, this works out with you in the new band, and it could be permanent. Meant to be."

Rave stared at him for a long time, thinking of herself five years ago, how she'd begged for this. Music had been her altar, the brothers her gods. They'd played Frankenstein with all of her parts until she'd forgotten that she had existed before them. Her throat, conquered. A colony laid upon her vocal cords. They took what she had so deftly that when they returned it to her in rations, she always felt the need to say thank you.

"This was mine," Rave said evenly. She bit back the tears welling and threatening to pour over. She wouldn't give him the satisfaction. "You got to move on. Dice got to move on. Why can't I?"

Ensley seemed bored now, and rather befuddled. He really thought he'd done her the biggest favor.

"We *are* moving on, love. Where've you been?" Ensley's expression went vacant as the Dog of the Hair's doors swung open, and his brother's music blasted into the night. "Now, c'mon. Almost showtime."

He was gone, and suddenly Amira was there, and they were bent together over the sidewalk like very sad contortionists. Rave cried hard and heavy into Amira's elbow, smudging all of her eye makeup in a way that still seemed rock and roll and then forced herself to stop.

Amira tucked a braid behind Rave's ear. "Hey, come on, if we hop on the train now, we can still catch some bad reruns. Get some takeout."

Rave exhaled, vision blurred. "What do you mean? I...have to go on."

Amira hiccupped in disbelief, holding Rave at arm's length. "You can't be serious. This was your first solo show since the band split up. As Rave and no one else." Amira paused. "No one *else's*. If you go up there with the Crooks and Thieves, you'll be reduced to a sideshow. A pixie attraction..."

Rave had gone still, tuning her wings.

Amira grabbed her arm. "Rave, they're playing chess, and you're the pawn. Ensley doesn't give a shit about your career. He knows that the crowd wants *you*, so he has to have you."

Rave massaged her own temples. "Amira—"

"He knows that Dice will see you up there with him and lose his mind over it. It's just a *game* to him, and *you're* the one who's going to lose. I can't watch you do this to yourself again and again."

Crescent moons sprouted in a row on the inside of Rave's palm. When she pried her fingernails out of them, they dripped blood.

She could not look at Amira when she moved past her. "If you can't watch, then close your eyes."

when the children cry

Rave is a young girl. Underneath the suburbs, the houses are picket; the fences are stucco. When the band splits down the middle, she is torn in the center, and the boys at either end of her make it out alive.

Everyone mourns The Scarlet Three. Posters are ripped and stuffed in garbage cans. T-shirts are burned.

It starts slow. There are rumors that Ensley had been in love with her first, then that Dice was. That they were both in love with her. That neither was in love with her, but she was obsessed with both of them. Perhaps all of those things had at one point been true.

Rave is walking home one night and on a telephone pole, she sees one of their old gig ads. Ensley and Dice are gorgeous. Someone has drawn devil horns at her crown, a mustache above her lip. Across her chest, they have written YOKO.

She never tells Amira the gory details of what forced her over ground.

She just wipes her nose and stares down at the wanted roommate ad. "I was in a band. We broke up. I'm just...looking to start over."

Amira smiles at her for the first time, and Rave understands the sun.

"Anything I might have heard before?"

Rave shakes her head and smiles a little, too. "No, we were very...underground." They are chatting over drinks, and suddenly she is telling Amira about the brothers, how they chose her, how she's become a shrine of blame.

Amira is quiet and gentle with her next question. "*Was* it...because they were in love with you?"

Rave laughs and just can't stop. "It started because of a song lyric." She snorts and it's infectious; Amira begins to laugh, too. "Dice. He wanted us to sing a song called 'Rolling the Dice.'" Amira laughs harder, and all of Manhattan quakes with their joy. "But nothing rhymed with Ensley. And that made him *so* mad."

It takes them awhile, but they finally sober up, and Rave is already memorizing where she'll live for the next two years.

"No, it didn't have anything to do with me," Rave says, "it was because they're in love with themselves."

gimme shelter

The kitchen had always been their No Man's Land. Amira was always making something good, and Rave was...always hungry. After their fight, after the show, she returned to a dark apartment. The walls seemed tight, like even they were disappointed in her, like Amira had told them what she'd done.

She sat at their counter until Amira stumbled sleepily into the hall, en route to the bathroom. She paused, back turned to Rave, shoulders tense.

"Was it okay?"

Rave nodded, even though Amira couldn't see.

"I love you," Amira said then, and Rave's wings perked up, mimicking an angel's choir with their strums, "but you didn't earn these wings to help those boys fly."

Amira came out of the bathroom a few moments later to sit with Rave.

"What are you thinking about?"

Rave peered at her. "Natural disasters."

"Cheery."

Rave shook her head. "We curse Mother Nature or God or whatever the Hell you want to call Her for natural disasters. As if she suddenly decided to strike. As if she's cruel for simply being. As if she hadn't had her plan all along before man decided to tread across it."

are you gonna be my girl

The night of Dog of the Hair's Battle of the Bands, Rave did not dream. She felt more awake than she'd ever been. She and Amira arrived late and wore little. Amira donned a gorgeous white gown and wings she'd made herself. She was surprised to earn a few smiles from passersby.

Rave wore scarlet.

9:05pm

"I want to sing with you. Tonight."

Before Dice could respond, Rave smiled and raised a glass to his lips. Vodka. Straight vodka.

Dice tried hard not to wince as he gulped it down, but Rave could see it behind all the grin and hair grease.

236

"Yeah?"

Rave nodded. "Yeah."

<u>*11:08pm*</u>

"You're right, this should be permanent."

Ensley smiled, trapped her against the wall in the cage of his arms, but for the first time, she did not feel claustrophobic. She felt like a prisoner with a copy of the key.

"I *miss* the band," Rave cooed, "I miss you."

He seemed satisfied, but not surprised.

Rave raised two glasses. "But first, cheers to us."

Ensley coughed at the whiskey.

Strange.

Rave's water tasted just fine.

<u>*9:15pm*</u>

"One more drink, one more drink!"

The Leather Bullets, Rave included, chanted around Dice in a circle, as if his ego was a demon and they were summoning it.

Rave stood back and watched, still as Holy Water.

<u>*11:19pm*</u>

"Are you sure? We go on at midnight." Rave held the glass back from Ensley, still *just* in his reach. She took a few punches at his pride. "You know that you were never good with whiskey before a show."

"Give it here," he practically growled, emptying the glass almost as quickly as she'd poured it.

9:50pm

Dice was swaying from foot to foot, trying very hard to focus.

"I talked to Joe about midnight. Prime spot, just for us."

Dice smiled. "Not ten?"

Rave shook her head. "Not ten."

"Wicked. Knew I kept ya 'round for a reason," Dice laughed. He turned to the band. "Let's have us another round then, lads!" Their shot glasses hit the counter all at once, drowning out the sound of a final call for The Leather Bullets to the stage.

midnight

There was whispering, and the crowd was thickening. Someone was faceless and calling her name. Rave felt mythic. Dice staggered towards her, her very own false idol.

"Y'think I don't know what ya did?"

He was sloppy and loud, but his voice cracked like a young boy's on every emphasis. Rave backed into Amira, who placed a finger through her belt loops, anchoring her to shore.

"I don't think anything about you," Rave said evenly, "ever."

Ensley appeared, too. They could both barely make it up the steps to the stage, shoving and punching at each other in all the confusion, then, for the first time in years, clinging onto one another for support. Perhaps in her revenge, she'd also done them a service.

"How is it that I'm on now—"

"—when I'm on now," Dice finished with a slur.

Rave pretended to contemplate this. "You're right, that *is* impossible. I must have been mistaken. *I'm* on now."

Ensley called her something awful under his breath, and she took it as a compliment.

"*Burn*," Amira mocked, helping Rave up the steps, parting the boys like Moses.

brown-eyed girl

Rave is a young girl.

That is the point. Rave is a young girl. With many faces and one spirit, living deep in a hut at the root of every story. Behind the battle. Beyond the crossfire. Pressed to the wall of prose by action like wallpaper, alabaster. The stage of it. The heart of it. The Helen, the Yoko, the Eve.

These stories unfold like window displays. Guns and swords and crisscrossed guitars fill our eyes like Christmas lights. But it is our duty as voyeurs of this world to press our faces against the glass and beg the story for its young girl, to ask what is happening to her, what is transforming inside of her, the real tale and not just a trick of the light. The way she decays, the way she floats down the river, the way she shouts with her mouth closed, the way she paints her claws, the revolution caged inside of her bones.

The way she falls in love with another girl.

While everyone wonders which boy will win her.

free bird

She takes the stage, and the room shares one set of eyes. She is burgundy and gold and something to be revered. Her braids rival Medusa's mane, wings outstretched and tuning themselves.

Ensley spits blood.

Dice shoots him a look.

Rave presses her lips to the mic, and from deep in the center of the crowd, Amira parts hers as if she is being kissed.

Rave sings.

hero to a god,

running out of time.

I want to kiss your lips

and die divine.

A siren's song. Amira's body beckons forth and even the most rigid bend for her passing. The spotlight finds her body and acts as the Red Sea.

natural disaster,

run for your life.

whole earth broke

the day I called you mine.

Rave kneels at the edge of the stage.

I told you

I didn't love those boys.

HALLOWEEN

this season in which we can pretend
to be something other than ourselves
in order to finally be ourselves.

for one night, gruesome is delicious and allowed;
we can be careless with each other
and not apologize in the morning,
blame it on all the people we can't possibly be.

once a year:
the bones, the blood, the cobwebs.
the gift of getting to choose what we fear.

how are these costumes anything but honest?
anything but what we are dying to be, what we know we are?
scary, slanted, impossible things.
the queen of hearts cannot handle her own,
the sailor resurrecting what was lost at sea.
do we not drain each other without teeth?
do we not haunt each other without white sheets?

how I wish that you would always show up at my door
with a pitchfork and red horns,
so that when I kiss you, I know exactly
what I'm delivering myself to,
exactly what will need to be exorcised from me
when you leave.

WISH UPON

why are we taught to fear
the beasts
and wolves
and witches
in fairytales?

would you not rather have me like this,
true with my intentions,
cursing you with my legs spread?
kissing you with my teeth bared?
loving you with my magic showing?

would you not cut me open with the glass slipper,
would you not eat the poison I have to offer,
would you not drown yourself to breathe like me?

SOMETHING WICKED

we are not the witches you are afraid of.
we are worse.

we were birds in flight,
so you gave us beaked noses.
you were envious of our magic,
so you saw us in green.

you believed we rode in on
the brooms we used to clean up your mess,
so afraid of enchantment
that you burned us to the bone.

but we do not flock from the west,
we burst from the earth,
midsummer queens,
starflowers bending towards the moon.

incantations murmured into coffee cups,
one eye, two eyes, a third eye,
handkerchiefs unfolding into spell books,
hair cloaking us like weeping willows,
dressed like the wings on crows,
silver rings stacked heavy on skin,
dancing until we are without feet.

we are not the witches you are afraid of.
but you should be.

WHEN A WITCH FALLS IN LOVE

when a witch falls in love,
the crows worry,
the moon is jealous,
the roses wilt.

you become the altar upon which
she lays all her blessings and
her curses,
summoning something immortal
from the parts of you
you'd laid to rest.

in her eyes, you are a match
striking against the book of her skin,
mouth spitting gasoline,
the feather of a phoenix,
the bite of a dragon,

unable to distinguish between the fire
that was already inside of her
and that which will be her end.

GODDESSES LOVE GODDESSES

you fall in love with her, and it kills you.
but you still visit the temples,
you still sacrifice your skin.

Persephone wants the garden of your body—
every winter massacres the roses,
every spring massacres you.

Medusa just wants you
to look her in the eye,
and it's a kind of suicide
when you believe that it'll be different this time.

Aphrodite wants you by the window
with your shirt off, mouthful of poetry
that gets lost in translation
on the way to her tongue.

Athena wants you holy and golden
on the floor of the woods,
making love to the sound of the
war in your mind.

you fall in love with her, and it kills you.
on your knees,
hands folded in prayer,
legs spread in sin.

when the gods open you up,
let the right one in.

IN THE REALM OF FAIRIES

dear mother,
I'm sorry that I never came home for dinner;
my belly was already full.

dear mother,
you always told me that I would become
something awful if I ate the fruit.

but now I think the point
of the story is that if you chose to eat the fruit,
you were already something awful.

dear mother,
I want to be the kind of thing
that the darkness fears.
when I laugh, I want black magic
to spill out of my mouth like blood.

from their backs spring bat wings,
from their hands, poison berries come to harvest.

the night court swims
in a river of limbs,
teeth,
and red wine.

dear mother,
in it, I open my mouth
and pick the fairytales out of my teeth.

dear mother, I ate the fruit.

sincerely yours,
something awful.

LAST NIGHT, THE COSTUME PARTY
(after Rebecca Tamas's "Interrogation")

And of the flapper?
I still have her pearl necklace.
I still have the taste of champagne in my mouth.
Just to be clear, the pearl necklace was a noose.
Just to be clear, her mouth was the flute.

So she was deadly?
Deadly.

Deadly enough to—?
Is exhibition the opposite of prohibition?

What I'm saying is, do you think—
Or are they partners in excess, too?

And of the pirate?
Sea foam and whiskey, the stench of it.

And of the harlequin?
They say you found face paint underneath the victim's
fingernails.
They say that she died smiling.

I can't disclose that information.
You can't disclose the truth to find the truth.

And of the devil? What about the devil?
Which one?

The man who came to the party as a devil.
Don't we all?

And of the vampire?
No one runs screaming on Halloween, that's the problem.

And of the ghost?
See, so much is frightening that nothing is at all.
Everyone can finally be who they are.

And of the mummy?
Would it be in poor taste to keep that under wraps?

Sir—
Okay.

Sir—
I didn't see them.

And of you?
Yes.

Amongst horrors what horror were you?
Myself.

BAD BLOOD

whoever said that
reincarnation was romantic,
never picked eighteenth century gravel from their teeth.
call bruises birthmarks (I still remember you).

first,
we were god's children, and I wore my birth
like peach and pink; you sunk your teeth into me,
a sinner.
in this one, you were the serpent
and I mistook an apple for glory.
I stared down the line of your pointed finger,
realized, your rib is the worst part of me.

in another legend,
you were a monster and
I was a lady who understood your growl as a song.
we were beasts, and this was our beckoning,
until I rose too high on your bramble throne
and called down to you, "eat your heart out"
but you ate mine instead.

in the next century,
I was a queen and you were my knight
made of iron and shadows,
reached out and caught me
on the hilt of your sword,
traitorous and trembling and as I lay dying,

you laughed and said,
"a lion's heart still belongs to a lion."

I met you again in a nineteen-twenties speakeasy;
and your grin cut like bones

(what did Caesar remember
when he saw Brutus at the gates of hell?)
I pulled my gun, but you were too fast,
wrote my death until I was
all blood-soaked diamonds and feathers.

(the answer is everything)

tonight, the room thrums and you hoist me up
against a dirty wall, kissing each other's necks
with knives to the back of them.

in every lifetime, I love you.
in every lifetime, this makes you laugh.

HEARTS, DIAMONDS, CLUBS, SPADES

before she was your scarlet queen,
she was a girl made of bread and velvet,
from a very small village with a very big heart
and her smile set your old wicker bones on fire.

you told her, *I can show you the world*
but never asked her once
if she had already seen it.

you thrust her into a game of
crowns and thrones and thorns,
fed her that big heart,
kissed her knuckles bruised,
and taught her words that only men should say.

(the audacity of painting her red,
then blaming the canvas)

but the years tarnished her novelty
and there were other girls made of
dandelions and thread,
wine and the moon,

and in those years, she grew raven wings,
black as night,
skin the color of battle paint.

in those years,
her bones raged a war against her skin
and ideas were born from dresses the color of blood.
they called her wicked, called her witch,
and other compliments,
until you couldn't recognize that maiden anymore.

and as she stood over you with a knife in her hands
and a wolf where her face used to be
in the second before you realized you were bleeding,

all you could think of was a joke you once told her
when she asked you, soft and innocent,
if she ever had a chance to rule.

you laughed,
called her princess or sweetheart or little girl,
and like a tarot, read your own fate.

"then you'll have to
shed your skin,
shed your death,
shed your king."

on justice

A NURSERY RHYME

girls with horns, girls with hooves, girls soaked in soot,
girls with their spines bent, with their chests bared to the fire,
bad girls, horrible girls, revolting girls with their fingers
bitten down to the bone.

(the moon has its belly full)
let the pomegranate paint your cheeks like blush. like blood.

girls like medusa, turning men into stone.
girls with their eyes rolled back into waxing moons,
who aren't waiting for your return,

(are you still waiting for a sign?
this is a summoning)

girls who want to watch everything burn.
girls who impale themselves on your sharp wit,
claw out from the riverbank pulsing with freshwater,
girls naked and bathing in stars, turning rocks into thrones.

(retribution for Andromeda, retribution for Ophelia,
retribution for Joan)

girls with wicked intent, girls with bloodshot eyes,
with their fingerprints on the guns,
with their hands on the knives.
girls who became monsters, who were always monsters,

(who are something worse)

girls with an ugliness, with a vengeance,
girls who locked eyes with the devil
and felt only thirst.

STRANGE GIRLS AND WAYWARD WOMEN

I love strange girls.

Sometimes I think I am just a collage of every strange girl I've ever seen, admired, touched, and met. *There*, she lives in my left pinky. *Here*, she resides permanently in this spiral curl.

I clung to them like their eccentricity could be contagious. Moved purposefully to brush elbows with the blue-haired lady on the train. Shadowed Amelie Poulain's venture across Paris when I studied there, sat in every photomaton with her cinematic ghost. Knelt at each altar to Frida Kahlo, pressed my face into a book of her paintings and breathed in, hoping to inhale the fumes of the ink of the press of the decades of the heartbreak of the very first brushstroke.

I love the odd ideas and ferocious whims, patchwork dresses and skinned knees, odd facts spilling from gentle lips— *perhaps not so gentle lips.*

Beyond the quirky archetype that lives in films and books and belongs to men more than it belongs to us—a genuine peculiarity, a disconcerting curiosity, a strangeness not for the sake of the world, but in spite of it.

In a city of closed mouths, the teeth; in a town of pickets, the wrought iron fence.

I love strange girls, mostly, because we are all strange girls. Even the pleated skirts and polo shirts, the highlights and pumpkin spice. There must be an extra vein you're born with when the world is so desperate to bleed you dry. You must be so much when it spends a lifetime trying to convince you that you are just one thing—sexy, maternal, over-emotional, crazy, cute.

I made a pact with myself to only ever write strange women. And in doing so, I might only ever write real women.

Why her tooth is chipped, why she gave that newspaper stand off the highway in Hughes, Arizona a second glance, the way she lines up the plates for dinner, the color of her favorite pen and what she thinks about it.

If you want to know what happens to her, you must get to know her first. You must meet her with your own eyes; I will not allow you to borrow those of the man who loves her, hates her, really wants to screw her.

Every poem, a call to assemble. An SOS. *Testing, testing, Radio Metaphor.* I am sending out similes like flares into the night. I am stranded in idiosyncrasies, isolated on weird girl island. In this stanza, *are you there?* In this verse, *can you hear me?*

In other stories, my league of wayward women gamble but hate to barter, always need something tied around their wrist, talk to themselves in made-up languages but the words are not words and they always mean something different. They sit around me in a circle—real faces and paper skin—and call me home.

We're here.

We got your signal.

We heard you.

GIRLHOOD

it was the summer we all wanted to die.
it was the summer we were all terrified to go outside.
with their masks on,
with our blood ready,
it was the summer of scream: don't go out after dark,
don't make eye contact, don't take your jacket off.
ready? begin.

it was the summer my bare midriff became a mating call.
this morning,
I passed through a line of construction workers, wading
through the shark's den
like my body had some debt to pay for being.
the slits of their eyes, the token of my flesh.

I am not new to this race
to be the final girl,
turning on my sisters
just to stomach a turn with him.

the horror movie Madonna,
soul stolen
then dangled over my head as a prize.

it was the summer we became so sad,
it was the summer the princes decided
to catcall us back to life.
break the spell,
come on baby, smile.

it was the summer we gave up our hearts
in the black market of girlhood,
traded them in for hotter blood
and thicker skin.

parts of our bodies that had not yet been
touched with permission fondled in the hallway,
smiling goodbye to dignity,
shed like petals off snatched flowers.

it was the summer I had to learn how
to survive despite him,
and he just learned
how to survive.

CRUSH

my body as a hotel.
my body as a building.
my body as a building,
and I get to live in every room.

how I used to exist with my windows open,
my doors wide,
always wanting to let the light in;
never understanding that free entry
meant for everything.

a resort,
a bed and breakfast,
a motel on the highway.
I was once a sparkling destination.
I let too much in.
all the kinks straightened,
all the strangeness painted over.
I decayed and became
just a place to stay.

all the men all the parents all the pain
that graffitied my throat and still
vandalize the things I say;
all the footsteps across my heart,
and cracks in the walls like scars on the skin.

how I used to exist outside of myself
to become a home to everything.

my body as an abandoned building,
and I, the woman who haunts its insides,
shouting at trespassers.
too much happened here;

I am afraid you will take even what
I barely have left.

how my eyes used to light the city and invite guests,
how my posture used to blanket me in stars.

my body as a home,
my body as a fireplace and warm hearth,
my body as my body and nothing else.

GIRLS LIKE US

girls like you are dangerous,
he says as he touches my throat.
I can't breathe, and I call him Columbus
on the plains and mountains of my pride
claiming what was already mine.

girls like you are dangerous:
tattoo it on my elbow in iron and fire
so that it scalds him when he touches it.
you'll break some poor boy's heart one day;
I imagine he also thinks Helen
started that war.

girls like you are dangerous
those eyes (the better to—)
that skin (to—)
those lips (to eat you—)
I am a wolf, you let me in.

girls like me are dangerous,
are soft
are terrifying
are beautiful
we are intergalactic, star-fire,
celestial—

and the galaxy didn't ask
Armstrong
to leave his mark
on her moon.

INAUGUARATION DAY

in my dream,
snow white wakes up,
unclenches her fist,
and tells the prince that she doesn't want to be kissed.

she demands to be known by the fire
raging inside of her,
but she is porcelain, and they name her so.

the more breakable we are,
the more beautiful we become.

in my dream,
I choose to be hideous.
I open my mouth and from it spills
a tangle of thorns,
a wolf choking on the full moon,
heat and blood and angles.

in my dream,
they burn my sisters and I at the stake
for having the tongues of witches
and we smile when we complain about the chill.

we build our homes
on the pavement,
the front of the bus,
the edge of the Nile,
the bottom of the vial,
hug ourselves to feel the earth.

in my dream,
we do not rewrite history;
when they bend us over,

we reach for the future.

on our knees,
we gather the soil from which
our daughters will grow.

in my dream,
we are Dorothy,
we are the wicked witches.
we keep our knives ruby red and sharpened,
aimed at the man behind curtain,
and march forth.

the wizard will see us now.

SAY HIS NAME

when he fell,
was it easy to call him Icarus
when you knew he was the sun?

everyone knows Sisyphus for his boulder
and Atlas for the bend of his shoulders
and not the boys who were boys
before they became kings.

a body built for war,
a heart thrumming for more—
which do you think will leave a legacy?

they lay him down in dirt
and will remember him as charcoal
and the splatter of blood
instead of paint.

a rose for its thorns,
a plant for its prickle,
Patroclus for his limbs.

he changed the world
in one million ways,
but all that's left is the story
of how it tried to change him.

YO SOY

I am not your feisty or spicy
mommy (it's *mami*)
or your flavor of the month
or your Bronx souvenir
or your gentrification compensation
or your Polly Pocket Jenny from the Block

> no soy tu chica luchadora o picante
> "mommy" (es *mami*)
> o tu sabor del mes
> o tu recuerdo del Bronx
> o compensación por gentrificación
> o tu Polly Pocket Jenny del Bloque

I am the plastic on the sofa sticking to the back of my thighs,
I am Sunday on the island in my grandmother's eyes,
I am a soundtrack of dominos sliding across linoleum,
the consistency of the coquí,
the song that was born in my hips,
and the sweet spill of Spanglish from my lips,
languages tripping over each other
on the way from my heart to my tongue.

> yo soy el plástico del sofá pegado a mis muslos,
> yo soy Domingo en la isla dentro de los ojos de mi abuela,
> yo soy una banda sonora
> de dominos deslizándose por el linóleo,
> la consistencia del coquí,
> la canción que nació en mis caderas,
> y el dulce de Spanglish derramándose de mis labios,
> los dos idiomas tropezando unos con otros
> en el camino de mi corazón a mi lengua.

by the way, I lied

you cannot roll your r's

you sound like a pirate

y por cierto, mentí

no puedes rodar tus r's

suenas como un pirata

IT WAS JUST LOCKER ROOM TALK

if boys will be boys,
then girls must be wolves.

if they are down by the reservoir,
killing each other with toy guns,
we must be one thousand Ophelias
floating upriver like the dead come alive.

the undercurrent of the man's tale,
knife in hand looking for hamlet, shouting,
I would rather be a fish without a bicycle
than a book without a spine.

if they are in the locker room, then we must descend
from the posters with our claws out and teeth sharp,
curl out from under their tongues and cut them off,
unbend from under their feet,

take back our skin,
take back the streets.

if boys will be boys,
these girls won't be sweet.

GIRL GANG

they come out at night
with clenched fists,
smiles like tight leather
and mouths dripping blood—
hair and hips swinging,
desperate for a fight.

hanging over barstools and running like
desert storms, shouting,
"I keep falling in love with the same bruised fists"
and
"no tomorrow will compare to this."

gory, pretty fault lines
dirty, pretty things like the eye of a storm.
a coven of cackles;
a sisterhood of travelling sins.

yelling,
"I am where the world ends"
and
"this is the kind of trouble you want to get in."

they are hair-knotted,
sloppy-lipped, bonfires and caravans,
bandaged bows and tattoos shouting:
BOW TO NO MAN.

risen from sand and bled from heartbreak,
candy kisses, hooked elbows and
broken dishes, biker jackets
stolen from truckers, bathroom stalls
scrawled by girls in love with each other.

road dogs, passed notes and knives
both stained with lipstick and
angel cake.

if you're already running,
you've made a mistake.

CARNAGE

tell me what it's like to walk alone at night
to play the game and also make the rules
to be the warden of your own bones

like a child you begged to be the one to plant the seeds
not to tend but to collect
you liked the idea of them sprouting
you liked the idea of roses

but the thorns but the watering can but the labor

you liked the idea of them sprouting
then left them all to die

in this garden
sowing without tending is just
murder but use your inside voice
in other words
I reap what you sow

you are a hoarder not a hero
son of Christopher descendant of Columbus
confuse my insides for your brave new world
and begin the carnage
ancestors ancestors
we have walked this line before
you have always been mistaken
and I have always suffered the consequences

I don't need to look like your sister
remind you of your mother
do not need to be born from your rib
to exist without being punished for it

must I resemble what you also consider property
must I kill everything else in me that lives
even freedom is held captive

I was born screaming
must I unlearn that language
is that how I win

I WILL TELL THE GIRLS

I will tell the girls to think hard
before setting the store hours of their open hearts;
on pilgrimages they will come to me,
the old woman living in a graveyard of good intentions.

I will tell the girls to remember how the earth
bloomed when its people stayed inside,
to wonder how much of themselves exists as it exists
because of those who walk upon them,
that they will find themselves wholly in the things they hide.

I will tell the girls that they can grow in this
without pretending that it's beautiful.
I will hand them stone tablets,
and they will write their own commandments.

I will remind them to edit
their love letters for pleas,
that nothing will ever be seen sacred
to those who worship at their own feet.

I will tell the girls to listen closely
to what loss asks,
that every crossroad has a fist that will come knocking,
that every fifth month will turn a person into a past.

I will tell the girls to turn their bodies
into altars for their own bones,
to become their own homes,
to unfold their affection,
to hold memorials for their exes—

I will say, "this is what time does:
all the ways you still love them
are now just invented.

on places

ZEUS AND HERA VACATION IN PORTUGAL

I can tell you two truths:
Zeus cheats on Hera,
and they vacation in Portugal.

all summer, they spill Port
like blood.

all summer, they live
their myth as we do.

all summer, their daughter Eris
follows with a dustpan for the chaos.

all summer, she earns her fate
as the goddess of discord.

she stirs her coffee with his lightning bolt,
and at the restaurant he requests Julio Iglesias—
To All the Girls I've Loved Before.

MARRAKECH

Morocco is an amusement park for the senses.

In a small room overlooking a street with no name, only a small fan to usher in some hot breeze and a turtle mulling around on the hunt for pieces of tomato, the very old woman drawing my henna reaches a finger to curiously trace over my real tattoo, neither of us able to offer up a word the other will understand. Her skin is rough, but her touch is tender. She smiles at me, and the lines on her face are a map I don't know how to read. She smiles at me, and somehow, I do understand.

In the Atlas Mountains, the sand and smoggy streets take their reprieve. I walk upwards for hours in the wrong shoes, my feet coated in dirt and mud, my skin red from the exertion. But if this is a deal with the devil, he holds up his end. Green erupts from the earth, only that and sky. The air is cool, and a secret waterfall cleans a basket of oranges. The oranges are squeezed into juice, and a man offers me a piece of bread from an oven right there on the incline. Rain falls, then clears, and I see a white horse dressed in the most gorgeous rainbow coat, eating in a lush field. I am farther away from what I know than I've ever been.

Not everything has to be pleasant, it just has to be real. The smells of fabrics, the smells of rotten food, the smells of animals, the smells of oils, the smells of herbs, the smells of it all—like an assault, like an exclamation point. Some hissing and taunting, the sound of a prayer call like a song, the clattering and clanking, the honking motorists and whir of a world without stoplights.

The fish in Essaouira is so fresh that a tear spills when I bite into it. I think it might also be the wind. We're sitting on the rooftop of a restaurant right in front of the ocean. The blue is

blinding, and my mouth waters, all salt and substance.
Everything is like this in this country—the piercing mint, the
playful cumin, the fresh fruit. In all my travels I've learned
that the rewards come when you stop demanding places to be
anything else.

LONDON

I book a ticket, board a plane, and cross the pond. London is everything about New York underneath a magnifying glass. The gold glitters more, the grime is grimier. I don't find as many ghouls to accompany me on my journey as I had in Edinburgh. This makes me sad, but perhaps something is assuring me that at this moment in my life, I don't need to be haunted.

Every day, I drink tea and walk alone for hours. Every wall in Shoreditch shouts for my attention. I visit the Queen, but she doesn't meet me at the gate. I am surprised. I can't tell if I'm bored or calm or both.

On the final day, I find a park that has forgotten its proper century. Estates line one side of it, so gorgeous I feel like a vandal even staring at them for too long. I find a bench, and the sky is so open and grass is so wide that I'm sure I've stumbled into a painting. I start to cry.

WHEN YOU ONLY HAVE A FEW HOURS IN PARIS

— *Morning.* Walk straight off the Ponts des Arts and into the Colonade de Perrault where, if you stand on your tiptoes by some of the windows, you can peer in at some of the Louvre's statues without paying admission. It will feel as though the museum is telling you a secret.

— *Afternoon.* Wander through the Rodin Museum, all that human and stone being swallowed whole by the most gorgeous rose garden straight out of wonderland. Death and fresh blossoms kiss in this grove. You will immediately understand what this means.

—*Night.* Stand on the Pont Alexandre III and watch the Eiffel Tower for a while, beaming its lights across the city like outstretched arms. The gold and gilded green cherubs and gods will animate when you're not looking. In the hidden night clubs and trickling out of docked boats, trolls and wild things will stomp beneath your feet. Something electric, something too old and too new. This bridge was made for yearning.

IN THE BATHROOM STALL OF A RESTSTOP ALONG A ROUTE SOMEWHERE IN PENNSYLVANIA WHERE YOU CAN SEE EVERY DAMN STAR

I wrote,
dear Andromeda,

I am finally
unchained.

CONTINENTAL AFFAIR

they say that the best way to get over someone
is to get under someone else.
so, when they leave you,
leave, too.

relearn touch through the plane ticket's paper cut,
press your fingers into the earth and leave it quaking,
a seismic connection,
tracking the beat of your heart until it's
category eight,
leaving dead memories in its wake.

ride the road and let it wear a different face as you go;
the bartender,
the museum guard,
caricatures on the plaza,
the motel owner's daughter.

wear your nicest dress and let
the mountains wine and dine you,
one million miles behind you
down an aisle marked route 66.

wrap the atlas around your naked skin,
candlelight in the valley
while you dine in sin.

squint your eyes until you can't tell
the difference between lip prints and passport stamps,
lost in love, infatuated with the journey.

it's what you need.
it only knows how to keep going;
it doesn't lie.

PARALLEL

is there a space in time
for all the places my body left
but my soul wouldn't?

is there a universe in which I am still in San Francisco,
begging everyone not to tell New York about the love affair,
standing on the Presidio—endless and open—
dragged backwards in time by Haight Ashbury,
nature and art woven through the concrete and steep hills,
demanding to be a part of its infrastructure?

is there a universe in which I am still in Nashville,
with its heartbeat, pulse, and personality,
its hand jotting out in the darkness
to drag me onto the dance floor,
that crowned *me*, a Bronx girl, Queen of the Honky Tonk,
left me breathless by the stacked dive bars,
hot chicken nipping at my taste buds,
and the constant awareness that I was alive?

is there a universe in which I am still in Baltimore,
its spirit, its architecture, its labyrinth of secrets,
its patriotism cloaked in legend,
where I fled, suffocated by the stagnancy of my life,
and its blocks toured me through time,
docks still waiting for sailors from decades behind?

is there a universe in which I am still in Edinburgh,
where I first recognized myself as heroine,
witnessed street performers levitating, pubs exploding
with rich accents and the smell of warm whiskey,
where I watched over the city in silence,
possessed by queens past,
where I boarded a bus to the Highlands with strangers,

green hill magnificence, fairies trapped in jars
from a local shop by the lake,
where I threw myself into world
and found that it was waiting for me with its arms open?

is there a universe in which I am still under
Venice's enchantment, too beautiful, too impossible,
the gondola ride at dusk,
the mask shops as golden hour hit them,
where there were no cars, only water and alleyways,
and I raced through them like
I was being chased by adventure itself,
where I felt possessed, like one more hour
and I might begin to leak saltwater,
become bound by seaweed, trapped in the canals like a siren?

is there a universe in which I am still in Athens,
all ember and gold, demigods and glory,
built on ruins and reminding me: *I was all this,*
I endured all this,
and still came out shining,
revolving around a crumbling peak; tangoing in the streets,
candle glow and violinists at every soft corner?

is there a universe in which I am still everywhere else?
do the islands claim my skin?
does Beacon own my peace?
has Barcelona caught my tongue?
does New Orleans have me under a spell?

my want won't stop abandoning me.
have I left myself behind?

CUSP

when I leave a place,
I see it for the first time.

I say goodbye to everyone with my hands open,
grabbing all the things they couldn't give me
in their presence.

I eat the loss,
I dig through the absence.

this does not make me an optimist
or even an opportunist.

I'm afraid that I am this way.
I'm afraid that in death,
I will still be wanting.

on hope

LIFE IS A HALLWAY

The song was wrong, the movie was wrong. Life is not a highway. Nor a box of chocolates. How I long to write this with a sweetness, 80 miles per hour, the wind in my hair, and the sky in my mouth.

Life is a hallway. At least, I think mine is. Daunting and dimly-lit and always foreign, like a new home you don't fully adjust to until you're moving again. Every time I think I've caught up with my life, it's already sprinting ahead of me, another corridor lighting up at what I thought was the end of the hall.

I think I'm going about this the wrong way, charting and plotting and mapping, trying to figure out which doors to open and what might be behind them, how to cheat the journey and where the end might be—how to make it there without getting lost along the way.

When I think back to the happiest, most fulfilling moments of my life, they don't feel very strategic...or smart...or spectacular. In those moments, the hallway was just a hallway, and I didn't beg for it to be anything else.

NEVER LET ME GO

if I could go back
and meet you again at the beginning,
I would.

and I would not be cold.

I'm not mean, and I'm not aching.
honey, a part of me is still tender for you,
still soft,
still adoring,
still twitches at the lit-up phone screen.

but it's not about you,
not about any of it.

I simply love all women,
and so
I must protect even the one
you turned me into.

I would say:
I understand now.
I don't fault you.
I felt the same.
the view of hell must have been gorgeous
on the way into it,
all those flames before they burn us,
all those demons before they hurt us.

I would say:
here is a history book of our battles;
save us.
here is a roadmap of places
we were careless with our hearts.

don't pick up the phone on the night of August 21st,
it's when we start to fall out of love.

I would say:
god, I'd forgotten how beautiful you were
before being had by me.
when we walk away from the people we touch,
we must be walking away from ourselves.

I would say:
how could you love me already?
what you adore so deeply
does not exist.

I would say:
let's sit here for a moment.
I want to remember us this way.
we cannot want for anything
the way we want for strangers.

I would say:
let's walk away now.
the worst thing you can do
is get to know the person
you're in love with.

THE MIDNIGHT POEM

it's been too long
since I saw you last.

it's been too long
since I was someone
who could be loved by you.

at night, I stay up trying to piece together
the sound of your voice,
and I know that
I'm getting it wrong—

just a cocktail of sounds
from anything that's ever
been kind to me.

ADVICE

i. the human heart is a Halloween party;
so many things will come knocking at your door,
dressed up like love.

ii. you are not missing anything you chose to give.

iii. you are not missing anything they took from you either.

iv. there is such a thing as a moonbow—
a rainbow produced by moonlight rather than sunlight.
the source is different but the effect is the same.
should you kill your darkness or shape it?

v. stop excusing people for the things
that which you can't even forgive yourself.

vi. a rose does not ask permission to bloom; it just does.
practice calling your dreams your birthrights.

vii. first, the prince will do anything for you,
then only some things, then barely anything.
when the story ends,
make sure that you and the witch remain friends.

viii. although I believe in signs from the universe,
I also believe that the power is not held in their presence
but in our willingness to see them.

ix. acceptance is a tough pill to swallow,
but it's still medicine.

x. you're jealous of what's golden
but afraid to let the light in.

xi. let the light in.

IT'S OKAY

it's okay for dreams to fizzle out and fade like matchsticks. it's okay to have more of them waiting in the box, to strike one across emery and then blow it out. it's okay for dreams to leave in the night, to turn you tender, to look different come morning light. it's okay to not want them forever, to change your mind. it's okay to grow out of your dreams like too-small sweaters. it's okay to shelve them, to release them back into the world, to wrap and ribbon them—gift them to other people. it's okay to paint over them, reshape them. it's okay to want them back later. to show up at your dream's door with roses and a changed mind.

it's okay to never make some of them come true but still let them change you.

STARFIGHTERS

I hope the earth tells stories
of what we did here
and who we saved
on the tongue of a constellation

yelling,
I'm not sorry for the triumphs
we made in the dark.

or how we died like supernovas:
everything in existence
and nothing all at once,

and how space wore our scars
as craters and collisions
even after time forgot.

we were intergalactic ghosts,
sprinkled like dust coating the planets—
an armory of night.

(it's always been ironic,
how dark it needs to be
in order to see the light)

mother never taught us this:
if you want to touch the stars,
be prepared to burn.

EULOGY FOR A LIVING GIRL

my Rose of Jericho,
claiming as many lives
as this one will give you.

you've resurrected so often,
the graveyard dirt feels like silk—
a ballroom of beginnings,
a ghost waltzing
with all her futures.

waiting dream,
living nightmare;
your body is a coffin
where something has died
or is about to emerge.

THINGS YOU CANNOT DO WITH THE PAST

- change it

THINGS YOU CAN DO WITH THE PAST

- read it like a map
- fold it into an origami plane that will fly you towards the future
- let it rest. it has already done a lot of living for you. it is tired and retired, bought a vacation home in Florida. the future is gorgeous and waiting and wearing fresh lipstick.
- stop hiding it in the closet just to blame it for going rabid and trying to escape. tend to all its wounds and give it a good home. treat it kindly, and it will stop trying to hurt who you are now.
- call it a hero and not just who you were. celebrate it. march proudly through the streets, honoring that it died just to make room for this version of you.

IMPATIENT

years later,
I returned to our swing set,
I returned to our cafe,
I surrendered to the stack of old photographs.

finally, I understood Alice;
I felt ten times too tall.

time gets its hands on everything,
shrinks everything;
what had once been my universe
was now a set of miniature figurines.

the clock ticks:
you were not in love,
you were just impatient.

SECONDS

you worry you might not have time.
but a second just passed. another.

who knows about hours?
who knows about days?
months? years?

right now, we are soaked in seconds.
we are bathing in them.
overflowing. abundant.
there are so many seconds.

why don't we trust the grandness
of what is also small?

worlds were born in seconds,
ideas, dreams, thoughts,
lusts, disasters, prophets, hopes.
the universe just expanded. then again.

people are kissing for the first time,
remembering themselves,
children are opening their eyes
to their first sunsets.
you worry.

sometimes a second is all it takes.
take it.

TESTAMENTS

my heart became Eden,
my body became biblical;
your absence was my Genesis.

us,
some reverse creation myth.

you were Adam,
you were the snake.
you punished me,
so, I ate the apple.

I ate the apple,
and the heavens opened.

the heavens opened,
and it was the end of us.

it was the end of us,
and it was the beginning
of everything else.

ROME

I kept asking myself why.
why you left
why I hadn't
why we became what we did
why we cut the film before its ending.

and then I remembered a course I took
in college on why the Roman Empire fell.
we spent the entire semester trying to answer that question
and after neatly listing out every single piece of research
we'd obtained, every point in which one could have salvaged
the glory, my professor sat with our papers in his lap, marked
them all with a scarlet A, and said something along the lines
of,

"we ask ourselves why, but in the end, it still happened.
Rome fell, and a new era blossomed from it. we wonder
about Constantine, but we don't ache for him. we pose for
pictures in front of the ruins that were once on fire. there
were a million reasons why, and now there is only
acceptance. acceptance of what once was. acceptance of what
it is now.

have a good summer."

CAUSE AND EFFECT

I wish you could meet
the person I became
because of you.

timelines
are cruel that way.

I don't care as much as I used to,
but the point is that I used to.
I know that you don't care
at all anymore,

so I'm just trying to make the ghost
of who you were with me proud.

SHOULD YOU

should you ever open the wrong photo album
and lock eyes with my plastic ghost,
or take a sip of champagne on your new anniversary
and suddenly taste my tongue;

I hope you don't rip it up,
I hope you don't spit it out.

I hope you remember that it did not rain everyday
where we lived,
that sometimes there was laughter,
that there were gifts we saved from the fire,
that when you wake her with a kiss,
it is a leftover meal from
the bowl of what used to make me smile,
that we saw things with each other
that we will never see for the first time with anyone else.

that most endings were once really good books,
and that, in drought,
we were once grateful for this storm.

that we were just two people loving
the best we could
with the hearts we had.

we were kind to each other once;
let's be kind to each other now.

in finding the courage to move away,
one must not burn the old house down.

DEAR FUTURE

dear future,
what if I'm not sweet by the time you've had me?

what if when I show up at your doorstep,
my skin is weathered and my eyes are tired and
you can tell that I've spent my time
lusting after other probabilities?
that I was unfaithful to my fate?

dear future,
I will admit that I received your map,
but I've had a hard time understanding it.
(okay, fine)
in fits of rebellion, I tore it up,
in love, I let it be vandalized,
in the dark, I cried over it and smudged mountains into
highways,
ways forward into ways back,
so I've had a hard time understanding it.

dear future,
I've been circling the same dirt road and calling it home for
five years now.
do you still remember my name?
how much longer are you willing to wait?

dear future,
what if the years get their hands on me?
what if they forget that I am only borrowed
and bend my pages?
what if I arrive half-woman, claws in dirt,
less beautiful and more poorly assembled
than the delivery you were promised?

will you still want me?
will you still have me?
will you still know me?

dear future,
what if I arrive
and can't recognize that it's you
passing me by?
worse,
what if I never arrive?

dear future,
I keep begging you for answers,
and you keep answering in the sunrise.

HOMELESS GHOSTS

when the world ends,
the ghosts are left homeless,
the living wail louder,
and the future haunts harder
than the past.

their grand museums and
hulking barns and
abandoned ballrooms and
old victorian homes
are burning.

attics are all wreckage,
antique lockets are lost,
there is no history to hide in,
there is nowhere to unrest.

as such, they bury themselves in tomorrow,
they sink into the sea and pull down the moon;
they slip into the rocks and peek out as blooms.

at the end of everything, there is nothing to hold onto;
nor at the beginning of what comes next.
so, they neglect being fearsome,
so, they marvel, *look at all that you remember
when you are forced to forget.*

HALLEY'S COMET

A lot of time spent waiting for something to happen. A big love, a big chance, a big break. We all want the plot twist to fall in love with us, to choose us, to dress us in our own destinies. No song's more haunting than the ticking clock. "If only and when?"

But think of all the sunsets you didn't expect, the loves that were never love, were almost love, were still as sweet, the small story of today, all you did and said even if it was as simple as breathing.

We are all here because of the right combination of people doing the most mundane things, because of everything living simply living. The train station strangers, a bud dying to blossom even in the winter, your own face in the mirror changing just a little bit every time.

Halley's Comet is the only naked-eye comet that might appear twice in a lifetime. Once for some. Sure...something like that? You don't want to miss it. Just like you don't want to forget the stars that show up for you every night.

While I'm waiting for something to happen, it already is.

DEAR NAICHE,

I am writing this letter under the moon,
hoping that under a certain brand of magic,
the crescent will deliver it back to you
hundreds of phases
before this one.

I would like to believe that
any whisper you heard in the dark
that kept you running towards the light,
that any voice of motivation that seemed to come
from nothing at all,
was this letter making its way back to you.

that you were you because I am me.
that I am what I am because you were who you were.
that you survived because I am here now, waiting for you.

right now, you are sixteen,
and I am twenty-five.

in your twenties,
you will be afraid
you will be vibrant
you will break and soften and harden over your youth
somehow all at once
like a wild garden
being watched over
by its own roots.

there were nights
that the place I am sitting in seemed
like a faraway fantasy. you toyed with the possibility
of me but it never seemed feasible.

too many times,
you handed yourself over,
about to surrender.

you were a walking expiration date,
bird bones,
terrified,
bruised,
tired.
but don't go to sleep just yet.

let me tell you this.
in your twenties,
you will book a flight
and let another city get its hands on you,
adopt another history,
bones and thrones and highlands lush with
what has only grown
in your dreams,
and it will give you hope.

you will dine with strangers
and watch lights explode in the sky
and get on so many trains and planes
with no certain destination,
which will quickly become your favorite destination.

you will walk all night in your pajamas
to pick up alcohol and cigarettes and chips
from the bodega and no one will yell at you when
you trickle in at 1am,
sit on your floor
and nurse the dark circles under your eyes
with three more hours of that show you like.
it is not perfect, but it feels free.

you will book another flight and
see the ocean rolling past cliffs and mountains,
trees as tall as your ambition,
people with hearts of gold,
and it will give you purpose.

you will realize that home can be where you're going.
and so, you will go.

you will spend a lot of time on the road
and the new pattern of your life will develop in the form
of abandoned places,
diner food,
filled notebooks,
mist,
exploration,
soft kisses,
deep lipstick,
lace dresses,
boldly female,
boldly yourself,
loud laughter,
strange towns,
going, always going.

you will learn to live in your body
and order dinner without hesitating,
your skin will transform from costume
to cage
to kingdom.

you will see ruins and parks and glaciers,
rock bands, roller coasters, mountains,
you will end up in different states by midnight,
and it will all take your breath away.
you will create in yourself what you have craved in others,

so that nobody will seem indispensable
and nothing will come between you and the light,
jumping out of careless hands,
feeling the fear and doing it all anyway.

you will hold a book in your hands with your name on it,
another book,
and then another.
you will stop accepting that there is no staircase
towards the stars
and start building one.
an inventor, not a voyeur, of your dreams

your anger will become a phoenix,
only invited into your palace of peace
when it learns to behave.
flowers will stem from the ashes that life left you in.

new people will teach you
that there is kindness,
that not every place to rest
will be swept out from under you like a rug.
the storm will have to stop,
there will be a pit stop somewhere.
befriend forgiveness, and it will give you a break.

that anthem of screaming,
of burns,
of tragedy,
of abuse,
will become an old song,
and your experienced hands will remix it
into the sweetest melody,
recorded over by jazz hitting cobblestone,
your mother and brother making jokes
when you go to visit your old home,

your own voice saying yes to possibility
and no to familiar demons.

you will know yourself so well that a shift in the wind
will have nothing on the foundation of your beliefs.
you will treat yourself so well
that you will recognize in a second when someone else isn't.

people will enter your life,
and you will love them,
and they will leave, just like they are now.
I'm not saying that it doesn't hurt anymore,
I'm just saying that the years will make you stronger.
to yourself, you will become kinder.
no one will be able to destroy you,
for the love that you give yourself will be an armor.

you will still mess up,
have more bad days than good,
be too broke to have anything more than sleep for dinner,
come home from work with your eyes half-closed,
trip up and let your heart loose on the wrong field.
it will still be a struggle,
but it will be your own,
and the climb will be from a higher slope on the mountain.

you will feel less like a worn-out forgotten road
and more like an exhibit of memories
for the next person to adore even more
for all that it is filled with.

this all seems like fiction, I know.
so weird, this difference in perspective.
for you, this is all probably a dream come true.
but for me, it sometimes still feels like misery repackaged.
I guess that's why I need your eyes to appreciate it.

it's like
stepping back from a masterpiece
in order to really see it,
remembering when it was just a canvas and some paint chips.

right now,
you are crying in your room
and nursing fresh cuts
and skipping breakfast and lunch just to barely eat dinner,
looking at the scale like some sort of race
without a finish line,
you are allowing your body to be his and his and his
battleground,
taking on wars that are not your own,
leaving yourself with all the damage.
you are hurting so badly.
I wish I could be your friend.

you thought you would never make it here;
I wish I could tell you
about all the ways in which I'm still breathing.

it is so jarring to know that somewhere,
you are still hoping to get here,
while I've been carrying you
this whole time.

thank you for listening
and enduring what you had to endure
in order to be who I am today.
I am nothing without the bullets you took.

you are a ghost now,
shattered glass with which I was able to
create a mosaic.

thank you.
thank you.
you made it.
we made it.

in an easier universe,
I could go back in time, hand this to you,
avoid all the hardships,
watch scars fade away,
save us with all that I know now.

but then there would be no letter to write.
I would rather feel the rain after living in drought.
I would rather eat this feast after starving for ages.
that is the complicated, awful, beautiful travesty of life.
I had to be that in order to be this.
pain is a door
loss is a window,
and I have learned to thank it all
for what it has challenged me to turn it into.

hear only this:
it gets better.
it gets so much better.

teenagehood can feel like such a prison,
but beyond the break
life is worth living after all.
it is all worth it.

for now,
I will keep proving that true
and wait to hear from thirty.

forever yours,
Naiche

ACKNOWLEDGEMENTS

Thank you to my mother, who has read every poem and listened to every whim. I believe in magic because you gave it room to exist. And to my brother—everything I do is to make you proud of me.

Thank you to my friends, my family, and my friends who *are* family. I adore you. It is a blessing to be loved by you as I am.

Thank you to those who have followed my work from its beginnings: just a girl on a blog, sending all her feelings out into the silence.

Thank you to those who have encouraged my dreams, bought my books, come to my events, connected with my words, and had me on their stages. In this world, I never forget what a privilege it is to be heard.

Thank you to those who have hurt me, left me, or ever once loved me. I am grateful for what you were. I am grateful for what you inspired. I am grateful for the parts of you that are now seeds, growing something strong within me.

And thank you to my past self who once wrote in a diary: "One day, I will be twenty-five and none of this will matter. One day, I will be as dauntless as the books I love to read."

It doesn't.

You are.

Naiche Lizzette Parker is a writer, witch, and lover of magic from New York City. She has been playing with words from the moment she was able to pick up a pen, and although she dreamed of many careers as a child—doctor, ballerina, camp director—she soon realized that all she truly wanted to do was write about them. Now twenty-five years old, *Nesting Beasts* is the fourth book of her poetry career. Naiche currently resides in her Brooklyn apartment, where she conjures up her stories. She still believes that she was born with an abundance of words inside of her, and she's hoping to get them down on paper before her time is through.

naichelizzette.com   **@naichelizzette**

www.ingramcontent.com/pod-product-compliance
Lightning Source LLC
Chambersburg PA
CBHW070531120726
47909CB00007B/2100